VETS IN TH

The third in the outrageously funny series by the author of *It's a Vet's Life* and *The Vet has Nine Lives*.

At last Michael Morton means to settle down as a partner in his uncle's Knightsbridge veterinary practice and marry his snake-charming fiancée, Julia. But his plans are suddenly disrupted – Julia goes down with appendicitis a day before the wedding, and Michael is summoned urgently to America by the Duke of Alanspring. Once in New York, he gets involved in the zany activities of American animal lovers – not to mention the eccentric antics of their pets.

'Alex Duncan looks like becoming the Richard Gordon of the animal clinics.'

London Evening News

'The author's fast and furious pace never conceals a hard core of veterinary experience ...'

The Countryman

VETS IN THE BELFRY

Alex Duncan

A STAR BOOK
published by
WYNDHAM PUBLICATIONS

A Star Book
Published in 1976
By Wyndham Publications Limited,
A Howard and Wyndham Company,
123 King Street, London, W6 9JG

First published in Great Britain by
Michael Joseph Ltd.

Printed in Great Britain by
Richard Clay (The Chaucer Press), Ltd., Bungay, Suffolk

ISBN 0 352 39702 0

CHAPTER ONE

The Duke of Alanspring, dangling his champagne glass like a brace of pheasants, stood in the centre of a scrum. The women surrounding him looked Japanese, French, German and American under their mink hats or wigs.

My South American companion smiled. 'A cosmopolitan gathering, isn't it, Mr Morton? Astonishing, this migration from Washington to New York ... for a cocktail party. Seems the best part of the diplomatic set's turned up.'

'I'm not surprised.' The young man who had joined us was holding out his glass for a refill. 'Washington is pleased about the Duke's marriage and wants to ... er ... give expression ... What I mean to say,' he suddenly sounded like a very new Third or Fourth Secretary, 'we *had* the Duke ... well, the Duke and that greyhound of his lived at a dozen or so embassies for more than a year. If Mrs Egon Miller-Hundling hadn't married him my Ambassador would have...'

'Yes, quite.' Clearly, the South American had recalled that I was English. 'Naturally, Mr Morton, we're devoted to his Grace of Alanspring. One has the greatest esteem for your country, but you can imagine no doubt that a distinguished guest...'

'who stays for indefinite periods ...' the Third or Fourth Secretary's hand had become unsteady. The champagne was dribbling over his fingers to the Asian goatskin carpet.

'My dear Hummington,' the South American sounded sympathetic. 'We all know ... But you must remember, for an English gentleman the cost of living in American hotels is prohibitive. So ... one was honoured by the Duke's visit. It's just that a distinguished guest presents certain problems for which not *every* embassy is equipped.'

'You're right there.' The young Secretary's glass tilted towards the carpet. 'The government's cut our budget for the second time this year. They've left us no margin for contingencies such as ... well, the steak-consumption of a brute like the Duke's hound. The estimates...'

The brute, still the best-looking greyhound I knew, was quietly licking the champagne off the carpet. Apparently he didn't mind its being made of Asian goatskins.

'It's a shame, sir.' Masters, the Duke's manservant, had stopped to refill my glass and was staring at the dog. 'A whole year he's had that psychology treatment, has Grey Rainbow.'

'He's looking well on it.'

'To be sure, Mr Morton. But does he feel any better about rabbits and hares? Can't abide them. Goat, lamb, mink ... everything but rabbit or hare. The fact is, sir, we had an incident even today. A lady called on Madam just before the party. She takes her hat off ... I could have sworn it was made of mink ... and Grey Rainbow gets all queer. Trembling he was, all over. Well, you've seen him that way in England, sir.'

'I don't suppose you examined the lady's hat?'

'No need, Mr Morton.' Masters patted Grey Rainbow's head. '*He* knows rabbit when he smells it whether it's titivated to look like something else or not ... Well, at least his Grace isn't sending him to that psychological vet any longer.'

'Is that why he's asked *me* to America?'

'Oh no, sir. We've invited you on account of our new idea.'

It was my first intimation that there was such a thing as a new idea or any idea that was not concerned with the curious allergy afflicting the Duke's greyhound. Remembering the Duke of Alanspring's anger when one race-track after another had refused to let Grey Rainbow run I had not been surprised when I received a summons to New York. The Duke had always been admirably pig-headed; despite his scorn of horse-racing he had managed to win enough on horses to take his dog to America for psychological treatment. And despite his notorious lack of funds he had cabled a promise to re-imburse me for my trip to America. The only surprises had been that my Uncle and partner hadn't objected to my going, believing that my

6

journey would enhance the prestige of our veterinary practice, and that the Duke's circumstances had altered so drastically that I was beginning to think *I* wouldn't have to pay several hundred pounds for the privilege of visiting his greyhound.

The visit had happened to me so suddenly that the luxurious apartment in Central Park West, New York, the exotic cocktail-guests and even Grey Rainbow seemed a figment of the champagne I had been given ever since my arrival.

The cold, sunny March day which had just faded away among the trees of the park would have been the day of my wedding in London, if Julia hadn't developed acute appendicitis. And if Julia, probably mellowed by her operation or by the anaesthetic, hadn't insisted that my 'professional interests' must come first I would have stayed in London and brought her regular offerings of flowers and caviare. Julia doesn't care for grapes and chocolates.

Even when my Uncle had persuaded me that a consultation in America would enhance our veterinary reputation, even on my way to the airport, I felt I shouldn't have accepted Julia's self-sacrifice. So, naturally, when May Tinker insisted on talking to me the moment she sat down beside me in the plane I tried to discourage her. I wished she'd stop talking about her hamster; but there she was, tall, blonde, embedded in mutation mink and hung with a hundred pounds' worth of Baroness-Bonetti glass beads. The hamster, Mattie, was there too; and he shouldn't have been.

Mattie was not listed under 'Passengers' or 'Luggage', and when he emerged somewhere over the Atlantic there was what the air-hostess described as a disturbance. By the time we landed at Idlewild May Tinker had the sympathies of the male passengers, Mattie the admiration of the female travellers as well as his cheeks stuffed with pieces of my waistcoat. Since I had become Mattie's handler on the journey, his owner felt we had established a special relationship.

When the three of us finally got away from the customs

officers it was quite natural for me to deposit May and her hamster at her hotel. I was not even surprised to learn that she too had been invited to the Duke's party. Mrs Egon Miller-Hundling, widow of a detergent millionaire, newly the Duchess of Alanspring, had entertained many film stars such as May Tinker at her estate in California.

'Sonia looks just darling,' said May, beside me.

I made an effort to stop thinking of Julia and the plane and the hamster Mattie. I tried to look attentive.

'I sure am happy for her,' May rambled on. 'The Dook looks good. Tall men with white hair, they just knock me out. How old is he? Do you know, Michael?'

'No, sorry.'

'Haven't you got his age in your records?'

'It was his *dog* who was my patient,' I told her.

'Oh, sure. Well, I guess he's around sixty ... Sonia must be – let me see – forty-five. That's right; her kids are ... well, Vernon's still at college but Vera's finished school. She's all of eighteen, that kid.'

The 'kid' was standing beside her mother, looking like the Duchess's younger sister. Both were leanly elegant and both wore their red-brown hair swept up on their heads making their faces appear fragile and large-eyed.

'Honey!' The Duchess spread wide her arms and embraced the couple whom Masters had just shown into the room. 'Why, it's wonderful of you to come ... taking time off from rehearsals. Willard! Willard!'

The Duke lifted his head. 'Ah, Claire ... Tiger ... Glad you made it. Play going all right?'

'Gee!' May's eyes had become alert with professional interest. 'That's Claire and Tiger St George Clemens. His play is opening on Broadway next week.'

'*Three Corsets to Curzon Street?*' I asked.

'Yes. You know it?'

'I do.' I wasn't likely to forget hearing the first draft in that manor house at Craftly, in the room with the lilac and mustard striped walls and the black ceiling; hearing the new play while Chou-en-Lai, Claire's lilac-pointed Siamese cat, was about to have kittens. 'I suppose it's one of Chou-en-Lai's sons.'

8

'I beg your pardon?' May was staring at me.

'The cat Claire's wearing round her neck. She had a Siamese called Chou-en-Lai.'

'Oh, she always wears it. I guess it was Tiger's idea. The reporters are just crazy about that cat. Say, Michael, do you know the St George Clemenses real well?'

'I think so.'

'I'd like you to introduce me, would you? I'm through acting ... that job of mine in California is fabulous ... I'm through with the stage, but Tiger's first play was real great. Did you see it? *Three Brazeers to Bond Street*. Gee, it was great.'

While Claire was telling me of the colonial-style furniture she had been buying for their English house, Tiger listened to May, his full ginger beard astir with emotion.

'... But the scene that knocked me out,' May was saying, 'is the one in the first act ... Remember?' The new resonance in her voice made some of the diplomatic guests lift their heads and drift towards our group.

May settled down to acting the parts of both characters until at last she blinked her eyes, as if the footlights had just been switched on, and gazed at her audience. The audience looked stunned.

'Well, I declare...' The Duchess's efforts at restoring the normal cocktail-party noises flagged. 'It's ... your play, Tiger ... it's...'

'Profound, Mother,' Vera suggested.

'Why, yes, honey. I guess that's the word...'

'Obscure,' said a man, behind me. 'Brilliantly obscure.'

'What's brilliant about obscurity?' asked a matron.

'Ma'am, any fool can be lucid.'

Claire turned, and smiled at the speaker. 'The Americans appreciate Tiger's plays much better than our dear Londoners.'

'Prophet in his own country,' I muttered.

'How right you are, Michael ... You'll come to the première of course?'

'Well...'

'Oh, you must. I'll send you a ticket.'

'I don't know whether I'll still be in New York.'

'Sure you'll be here,' said Vera. 'Mother hasn't told you her plans yet? I guess they'll talk things over at supper. Willard's dog...'

'Strange.' Tiger absent-mindedly stroked the cat on his wife's shoulder. 'Claire, did *you* know this? One can know a man like the Duke all one's life without realizing that he's got the Christian name Willard.'

'Tiger's great,' whispered May. 'I'd never have thought of it that way.'

Masters offered us a dish of nuts. 'His Grace is called after his maternal great-grandmother, an American lady. Her parents came from England ... in the *Mayflower*, naturally.'

The Duke picked himself a brazil nut. 'Rubbish, Masters. We don't know *where* my great-grand-something mother came from.'

'Sir?'

'Get along with you, Masters. Better help Mr Hegel get rid of his hat.'

The guest who had just come into the room with his hat on disconcerted me somewhat. Athletically built, of middle height, with grey eyes and a thin nose that would have suited him better had it been half an inch shorter, he looked like a brother of mine – even a twin-brother. When Masters had persuaded him to part with his hat I noticed one difference – his hair, as fairish as mine, was cropped in a crew-cut.

'Why, you were right, Willard,' said the Duchess. 'They really *are* alike. Isn't it cute!'

I was beginning to feel embarrassed; but so was my double. While he was squeezing past groups of champagne-drinkers, spilling a glass here, upsetting a tray of savouries there, Grey Rainbow had begun to bark and impede his progress by jumping at his chest.

'Poor Rand.' Vera dumped her glass, and made for Grey Rainbow. She grabbed the dog by the collar, telling Masters to put him out in the hall.

The Duchess introduced my double as 'one of our veterinary surgeons, Mr Bertrand – Rand – Hegel.' She said she assumed we had lots in common, and left us to ourselves.

'You the guy from England?' asked Rand.

'Yes. Do you know why the Duke wanted me in New York?'

'No.' Rand seemed on the verge of choking for want of a new subject. Suddenly he noticed Claire's back and the Siamese cat on her shoulder. 'Gee!' His fingers got caught in Claire's straight blonde hair but eventually found the cat's ears.

Before I could warn him that Chou-en-Lai the second didn't seem to like his caress, the cat had shot out a paw and drawn the claws right across Rand's hand. He put it in his pocket as if he hadn't noticed the bloody marks.

'Temperamental, these Siamese,' I said.

'Sure ... all animals are,' he blurted out.

'I suppose that's why you're interested in them.'

'I guess so.' He sounded dispirited. I suppose the scratches felt sore. 'The trouble is ... I can treat animals, but they don't know how to treat *me*.'

'Hard luck.'

'They're as bad as people.' Rand responded to my sympathy with unexpected animation. 'Glad to see you when they're down, but no time for you once they're okay. Grey Rainbow's as bad as the rest.' The dog had sneaked back into the room and was sniffing Rand's ankles. He did look as if he were trying to decide whether to nip Rand or not. Rand, taking no chances, moved behind the record-player. 'And *I* treated him for constipation.'

'That explains it. He didn't like the paraffin you gave him.'

'It was better than the constipation.'

'Where's your surgery?' I asked him, for the sake of relieving his dejection.

'I haven't got a surgery. I figured if anyone could walk in on me ... with any kinda animal ... I'd be spending half my life in hospital. See that?' He pushed up his sleeve, neatly unbuttoned his cuff and exposed his arm. 'That's where a dachshund bit me.' He pointed to several crescent-shaped scars. 'That was a poodle; that – a corgi; this a pekinese; this a Persian cat; here a monkey ... That's not

11

all. Wait till you see my legs.'

I stepped close up to him, preventing him from rolling up his trousers. 'You must show me some time ... If you haven't got a surgery how do the animal-owners find you?'

'They always do ... They sure do in California. That's where I live. In Santa Monica...'

'Santa Monica!' Claire turned to us. 'Michael, you'll adore it in California.'

'Am I going there?' I asked.

'Of course you are. After Tiger's first night. Sonia, darling,' she linked arms with the Duchess. 'You won't forget, will you? We're desperate for a ground-floor apartment, and Willard *has* promised we can rent yours when you go to California.'

'I know, honey. But we haven't yet decided to go. You see, Willard hasn't had his check-up yet.'

'Didn't he have one about a month ago?'

'Yes, but that was his pre-marital medical examination. Willard's got to be careful about his blood-pressure, Claire.'

'It *isn't* high, is it?'

'No,' the Duchess smiled, 'it's fine, just fine. Do you know, the doctor said Willard's as fit as a forty-year-old.'

'Then why does he want another check-up?' Claire sounded slightly exasperated.

'*He* doesn't really want it. But one's got to be careful about blood-pressure. And I won't have him die, not while *I* am alive.'

'No, of course not. But you'll remember about the apartment, Sonia, won't you?'

'Don't worry,' said Vera, '*I'll* call you after Willard's seen our doctor.'

The guests were lining up, thanking their hosts for the swell party, the charming, the delightful party. Swarthy and fair diplomats, women in mink or sable coats with blonde or copper wigs on their heads were saying how great it was that the Duke had married an American and would stay in the States for good. Claire had plucked Chou-en-Lai the second off her shoulder and was putting him into her outsize handbag. Tiger was offering May a lift to her hotel.

As the lounge emptied three little dogs came bounding

in. At least, I thought I saw three black, brown-faced miniature English terriers, which made Rand Hegel slip back behind the record-player. I couldn't be certain of *what* I was seeing; since my breakfast in London I'd missed lunch on the plane chasing after May's footloose hamster; I'd missed the hamburger I'd promised myself installing May and hamster at the Algonquin Hotel, and I'd failed in getting myself a foundation of cocktail-bits for my champagne.

After a plate of clam chowder I *knew* I was seeing three little black terriers as well as Grey Rainbow. They were feeding on a special platform at the far end of the dining-room, well removed from Rand Hegel. Rand, apart from myself the only guest at dinner, told me the bitch was called Manila and the two dogs Castor and Pollux. True to their mythological namesakes, Pollux had a gift for boxing, usually with animals twice his size, while Castor was capable of giving any horse 'the run-around'; and Manila – well, the Duchess had called her after that exotic place because she almost went there on her first honeymoon but never got lower down than Japan.

Rand admitted that the three miniature terriers were quite reasonable animals. Unlike most creatures, who bit and scratched him, the terriers were content with growling at him. Manila especially was almost sweet-tempered.

As if to disprove Rand's opinions Manila decided to show displeasure. We had finished our chicken and cole-slaw, the dogs their steak, when Manila gave a high-pitched yelp and began attacking her pink dish. She pounced and shook it like a rat and within a minute her sharp little teeth had reduced it to a kind of lacework doily. To make certain that her performance had not remained unobserved she stuck the ruined dish over her face and made for our table. All we could in fact see was a wreck of pink plastic stalking towards us on fragile black legs.

The Duchess took apart dish and dog and scooped Manila on to her lap. 'You've given Manila a plastic dish again.'

'Yes, ma'am,' said Masters, collecting our dinner plates.

'She doesn't *like* plastic ... Well, Masters, after all there

13

are plenty of people who prefer eating off china.'

'Yes, ma'am. But I thought what with our dogs going to school soon maybe a little training now ... self-discipline as you might say...'

'Better leave that kind of thing for Mr Morton and Mr Hegel,' said the Duke. 'We'll have some cheese, Masters.'

'Honey,' the Duchess looked concerned, 'you wouldn't prefer that nice new sunflower cream-reduced spread?'

'Matter of fact, I wouldn't, Sonia.'

'Dr Bonblust recommended it. You *know* how he feels about animal-fats.'

The Duke, a large chunk of butter on his knife, hesitated for a moment and then resolutely slapped it on his biscuit. 'To hell with the cholesterol, Sonia ... It *is* cholesterol, Morton, isn't it? Thought so. Stuff that gives you heart-attacks. Not *me*, though. Eaten butter all my life. Brought up on it. Now, Sonia, don't you worry. Mustn't pay too much attention to all these new-fangled notions. All right for animals...'

The Duchess looked happier. 'Then you haven't changed your mind about the Abdul doctrine, Willard?'

'Not a bit. Go ahead, dear.'

Under the table Vera's foot touched mine. 'That's *your* baby, Michael. Yours and Rand's. Mother's just hipped on the Abdul doctrine.'

'Now, you two veterinary surgeons,' the Duchess sat up like the chairman of a chatty women's club, 'have you read the *Doctrinum Animalis Psychologicum* by Abdul Karim Kochbar?'

'Inaccurate,' muttered Rand Hegel. 'Don't know whether it's Latin or Greek, but it's inaccurate.'

'Mr Abdul isn't a linguist; he's an animal expert ... You *haven't* read his book?'

We both admitted our ignorance.

'Never mind. You'll soon acquaint yourself with Abdul's ideas. It's only a thousand-page book ... I happen to have a few copies right here.'

'Only thing I don't like about it,' said the Duke, 'is the *doctrine* business. When I was a boy doctrines were things that Popes and the like went in for; nowadays they're ten a penny. Some little politician says it would be a good thing to feed starving people and – blow me – next day the papers, television, what-have-you call it a new doctrine...'

'Sure, honey, sure.' The Duchess patted his hand. '*Now*, it'll take you two boys a day or two to read the Abdul doctrine, so I'll just tell you the main points. And I'd like to tell you what we have in mind.'

It was two in the morning by the time the Duchess had satisfied herself that we knew what she had in mind. By then the Duke was asleep behind the *New York Times*, no doubt soundproof by virtue of its thickness; Vera, her dark eyes fixed upon Rand, was lying stretched out on the Asian goat-skin carpet, and Rand's efforts at controlling his yawns resulted in an intermittent twitching of his nose or ears.

He came to life only when I assured the Duchess that I would go and see her estate in California; he promised to accompany me, and followed Masters and me to the guest rooms.

I had just taken off my tie when I heard a cry from the adjoining room. At the same time there were sounds somewhat like muffled drums. I dashed into the hall and opened Rand's door. At the far end of the steam-filled room I found a plastic curtain and behind it a shouting, squirming Rand. He was trying to dodge a sharp jet of hot water as well as six piston-like arms which were pounding him with tough-looking boxing-gloves.

'Turn it off!' he yelled at me. 'Turn it off, for crying out loud!'

'Come out!' I yelled back.

'Can't.'

His objection wasn't unreasonable. If he stayed inside the shower he was buffeted by the pistons; had he tried to come out he would have been scalded by the jet as well. I examined the panel of taps at the side and turned one marked CJs. It released numerous thin jets of cold water without turning off the hot. By turning a knob marked H the hot jet was replaced by a cold which at least enabled Rand to get out.

'Gee!' He staggered to the towel-rack and wrapped himself in a bath-sheet. 'Thanks . . . I guess this is the new body-culture shower they're advertising now.'

'Looks dangerous.'

'It *is* dangerous.' Rand dropped on his bed. 'Doctrines,' he muttered. 'I guess the guy who dreamed up this *shower* had a doctrine.'

When I finally succeeded in turning off the jets *and* the pistons Rand was asleep still clutching the bath-sheet to his chest.

I was less fortunate. I lay in my bed awake, wondering in *what* Rand and I were to co-operate. If I had understood the Duchess correctly she wanted to set up a dog-training school at her Californian estate. Rand and I were to apply the teaching 'doctrine' of the Arab sage who had written a volume called *Doctrinum Animalis Psychologicum*. He claimed that his methods had proved extremely successful with the dogs of the Sultan of Salem Asur. As far as I could see there was nothing psychological about the training except that Mr Abdul Karim Kochbar appeared to know all about bribing dogs into obedience with judiciously admini-stered tit-bits. He also seemed to understand the psychology of animal-owners with a desire to have their pets trained at a top-dog establishment. And what could be more top-dog than a Sultan's kennels in the Middle East or a Duchess's kennels in America?

The Duchess, with equal acumen, had chosen the name *Wee Souls' Sanctuary Inc.* for her new training-school. Admittedly there were others in California and in other parts of the States, but she had heard of none that con-centrated on *little* dogs.

The syllabus, she had told us, was to be conventional and according to the normal practices of the American Kennel Club members. Dogs would be trained for the C.D. (com-panion dog) and C.D.Ex. (excellent companion dog) certifi-cates. Thus each animal in training would have to pass three examination shows and receive 170 to 200 points. A dog was awarded one leg at the first show, two legs at the second and three when his training was complete. After passing the third leg the dog would receive its degree, a document with a gold-seal fine enough to be framed.

The Duchess considered that the Hollywood Dog Obedi-
ance Club dealt with too many large dogs as well as being
too far away from Santa Monica; and Thousand Oaks, the
jungle compound where animals were trained for the
movies, was too 'mixed' – dealing with lions, monkeys and
such-like as well as dogs. There was a 'real need' for the
kind of place she had in mind. As for the Duke, he felt that
Wee Souls' Sanctuary Inc. would provide a new training-
approach to his greyhound, perhaps even an opportunity
for undoing the work of Grey Rainbow's analyst if not for
curing the animal's allergy to hares and rabbits.

Towards dawn my thoughts became somewhat jumbled;
one moment I was aware of being in a strange room on a
hard bed, the next Julia appeared before me accusing me of
behaving in my usual dissolute fashion. Why was I pretending to her? In whom *was* I interested? In that ex-act-
ress May Tinker or the hamster Mattie? And why had I
promised to go to California? There was nothing the matter with Grey Rainbow; that dog simply happened to be too
intelligent to accept the ordinary greyhound's destiny of
chasing after the hare. The real reason for prolonging my
stay in America was neither Grey Rainbow nor the setting-
up of a *Wee Souls' Sanctuary Inc.*, but the Duke's step-
daughter. Could I deny that I found Vera attractive? It
wasn't necessary to look at the Duchess and her daughter to
know what kind of people they were; their home made it
perfectly clear; just look at those body-culture showers –
yes, and the bottle-openers chained to the beds in each bedroom.

Julia wasn't through with me when Rand took over; or
rather he was being taken over by the Duchess's miniature
terriers who were asserting their right to bite Rand before a
grand army of hamsters took possession of his scarred
body. When Rand fled into the shower I felt bound to
rescue him, but when I got inside Rand had disappeared
and it was I who endured the scalding water and the batter-
ing body-culture pistons.

CHAPTER TWO

'Hi! Know what time it is?' Vera put a tray on my bedside table and sat down on my feet. 'It's ten, Michael. Rand's up and waiting for us ... You feeling okay?'

'Yes, thanks.' If I had told her that I was feeling as weak as a pup recovering from distemper she wouldn't have known what I was talking about. With her shining brown hair bobbing about her back and her eyes as clear as if she'd been drinking lemonade instead of champagne Vera looked wonderful. If I hadn't remembered my night-visions of Julia I *would* have touched her.

'You look younger in pyjamas,' she said, thoughtfully. 'How old are you?'

'Twenty-eight.'

'Same as Rand ... Funny you're so much alike; it gives me that psychological feeling. *You* know.'

'I don't. What's it like?'

'Oh, a feeling in the stomach ... Here, you'd better have some coffee. You look like you need it.' She poured me a cup and pushed it into my hand. 'You *want* to see New York, don't you? Rand does. Well, I've planned everything ... but we're running late. Mother and Willard are out walking the dogs.'

A good many people were out, walking their dogs in Central Park – not entirely for the animals' benefit. It was a beautiful day, very cold but brilliantly sunny. Almost every apartment-house we passed looked as if it had been prepared for the state-visit of a foreign politician. Elegantly striped or gold-fringed canopies sheltered the way to the entrances and where the doors stood open uniformed door-men could be seen against backgrounds of massed spring-flowers, red carpets and rubber-plants. In contrast to all that lusciousness the clumsy square boxes outside some of the windows gave the façades of the houses a tenement atmosphere. We had walked about a mile towards Frank Lloyd

Wright's Guggenheim building before it occurred to me that those boxes were not cages for delinquent hamsters such as Mattie but air-conditioning contraptions. Another baffling feature of this Mayfair of New York was the token gardens in front of the ground-floor apartments. Measuring about five feet by ten they consisted of well barbered hedges surrounding patches of gravel or a couple of miniature trees.

'Do people sit out here in summer?' I asked Vera.

'Oh no, one *can't* sit in the street.'

'Vulgar,' agreed Rand.

'How about outdoor cafés?'

'That's different,' said Vera. 'You can see now why Claire wants to rent our apartment, can't you?'

'Not really.'

'It's on the ground floor ... ideal for animals. Of course, you're not supposed to let your cats and dogs jump out the window and use the front-yards as a convenience. But if you arrange terms with one of the under-porters ... Well, you can *see* the front-yards are clean. At the moment Claire and Tiger have a sixth-floor apartment, so Tiger has to walk Chou-en-Lai in Central Park. Say, what do you think of this?'

I had seen photographs of the building that housed the Guggenheim collection of paintings and sculptures. I could accept its outer-space shape, but Rand looked worried.

'Let's get inside,' he said, hunching his shoulders.

'Isn't it cute?' asked Vera, proudly.

'Cute' seemed a strange adjective for the massive corkscrew shaped interior of the gallery and the brutally powerful sculptures of Fernand Léger, but Vera had been right in taking us to the place. It had a soaring quality, a rebelliousness as refreshing as the frosty sunlit day.

Vera allowed us half an hour for walking the ramps which took us to the various floors, for seeing paintings by Kandinsky, Klee, Chagall and Modigliani, sculptures made of transparent plastic or wire.

'I kinda like modern art,' said Rand, coming out of his trance as we got into a taxi.

'You weren't bored?'

'Sure I wasn't. It does something to me.'

'Does it give you that psychological feeling?'

Rand looked at Vera with sudden interest. 'How do you know?'

'Oh, I always get it in the Guggenheim. That's why I keep going there. I guess it's the Léger sculptures.'

'I've got an abstract sculpture in my apartment in Santa Monica. It's made out of my old car. My dog, Bernie, used that car ... so when Bernie died I didn't want to scrap it. Sculptor I met said he'd do something with it. He had it squashed in a power-press; it's as flat as a picture now, and you can still see bits of blue leather from the upholstery ... and a piece of the glove-compartment with Bernie's teeth-marks in it.'

'I'd like to see that, Rand.'

'Sure. I'll show it to you soon as we get to California.'

The taxi had drawn up outside the Hotel Algonquin. Vera said we were lunching with May Tinker; and look! Wasn't the place just crawling with film stars? The woman getting into the elevator; wasn't she...

'Dawn Petrell,' murmured Vera, awed by the lady who was saturating the lift with her rose-perfume. Even I knew the name and that amused lop-sided smile. Mrs Petrell was the kind of actress described in obituary columns as 'the grand old lady of the English stage'. The younger, American, woman she addressed as Gay was undoubtedly her new daughter-in-law, a girl widely quoted in gossip-columns for declaring that – much as she loved her English husband – she would not set foot in England as long as her eight poodles were not allowed to accompany her without being subjected to the 'barbarous English quarantine laws'.

Gay had left seven of her dogs at home or in some place agreeable to them; the only animal with her was a white medium-sized poodle in a powder-blue coat embroidered with the initials D.A.F. I wondered what the initials stood for, and I wondered what the dog did about the leg-part of his coat when he wanted to avail himself of a tree.

'Poor things,' said Dawn Petrell, gazing at some framed advertisements.

'Who, dear?' asked Gay.

'Americans, of course ... Look at these! *Imperial Glove Company Inc.* ... and ...' she put a pair of gold-rimmed lorgnettes to her eyes and scrutinized the picture of an immaculate-looking man in shirt-sleeves ... *'Prince Paolo's skin-freshener for men.* Really, Gay, it's a shame ... your government *should* allow America to have a monarchy. Obviously, it would make people very happy ... Of course, your country is rather young; maybe you'll get your monarchy in fifty years or so.'

'Well, I declare!' Gay sounded outraged.

'And another thing,' continued Dawn Petrell. 'Why do they always play *Bells of St Mary* in lifts ... elevators? Well, not *always*; sometimes it's *Poor Old Joe*.'

I rather agreed with the grand old lady; the music was oozing from an invisible cranny in the lift – music so sweet, so uncompromisingly soft that it made me feel as if someone was patting my ears with a well-used, grubby powder-puff.

'There's music everywhere,' said Gay.

'I know ... even in the er powder-rooms. Why *do* they do it?'

'Well – it makes people work harder. That's been established by experts. And it's soothing to the nerves.'

Dawn Petrell gave the Chinese liftman one of her world-famous lop-sided smiles. 'If our fellow-passengers don't object ... could you switch off the er music?'

'Can't, ma'am.' The boy made a helpless gesture with his hands. 'It's piped.'

'Like water from ... a lake, I suppose?'

'Sure, ma'am. Only I can't stop it like you can stop water.'

'Oh, I *am* sorry.' The lift stopped, and as Dawn and her daughter-in-law walked out we could still hear her sympathetic, 'So sorry. What a shame. Those poor Americans ...'

May Tinker turned down the wireless, which had been beating out the madison, and went to work at the cocktail-cabinet. 'Better watch me, Michael. I'm going to make old-fashioneds. You said you don't have them in England ...

Cube of sugar, a couple of drops of bitters ... cube of ice, slice of orange, nick of lemon-peel ... now, fill up with Bourbon and put a cherry on top. Try it.'

I liked her cocktail, and I said so.

'Isn't my suite just darling? I just love the antique furniture ... There's no place like the Algonquin. The atmosphere...'

I thought there was even more atmosphere outside May's windows; I had never seen a more exciting view of the back of a house. The first ten floors had plain, grimy windows set in yellow brick – obviously a part that contained storerooms and offices. On the eleventh floor things began to happen to the building; the brick became finely textured and rose-coloured, the windows – in sets of four – were topped by Gothic arches and the walls between sprouted baroque pendants like giant lozenges. The building looked as if it should have terminated there. But no, someone had crowned the eleventh floor with a beautifully proportioned little Moorish temple flanked by Spanish-tiled cottages; and on top of the cottages squatted two great, round, rusty oil-storage tanks.

For the first time since my arrival I felt I really was in America. Nothing I had seen so far had as much casual charm and exuberance as that preposterous view from May's window. And all of it was soaked in the kind of sharp, saffron sunlight one sees in Italy rather than in England.

The architectural fantasy out there suddenly made me think of May's hamster. 'Where's Mattie?' I asked her.

'Oh, I guess he's around.'

'Not in his cage.'

'I put in a cookie. He'll go get it when we're out.'

The dining-room – all crimson tapestry, dark wood, soft lights and bright table-silver – made me think of the *Christmas Carol*, but the lobsters and steaks were unmistakably American and very good indeed. And the waiters talked to one another in Italian and Spanish, French, German and Russian – and that too struck me as pleasingly American.

After lunch we returned to May's room for Vera's beaver-coat and May's mink. The cookie was still lying in Mattie's

22

cage, untouched, and there was no sign of the hamster.

'We'd better find him,' I suggested, remembering the 'incidents' of Mattie's disappearances over the Atlantic.

May opened drawers and cupboards, Rand and I searched under the furniture, and Vera dismantled the armchairs. No hamster. May was about to report her loss to the management when we heard a scream some distance away. High up, on the parapet of the Moorish temple opposite us, a woman in scarlet robes was being slapped by a man – which seemed to have no effect on her hysterics.

Below her waving, outstretched arm Mattie was cautiously circumnavigating one of those large stucco lozenges, quite unaffected by the alarm his appearance had caused.

'Gee, he'll fall,' breathed May.

'I'll go get him,' said Rand, dashing out.

Mattie had stopped at the edge of a chipped masonry leaf trying to decide whether to use the nearest window-frame or a drain-pipe for his descent.

'Mattie! Mattie!' May had thrown open her window and was holding out a pink biscuit.

Mattie had chosen the drain-pipe and was slithering down, making good use of chipped bricks, staples and wires. Rand appeared at the window above, surrounded by several tough-looking men. May pointed downward. Mattie, having discovered a bunch of power-cables, negotiated the next two floors at speed. By the time Rand showed up at a window above, among a bunch of hostile looking girls, the hamster had reached the courtyard. All we could see was a tiny speck scooting across between crates, trolleys and trash-cans.

It seemed hours before Rand came back, tie askew, collar crumpled, and put the hamster into May's hand. The nasty scratch on his cheek, he told us, was his own fault; he'd goofed. He had gotten into a ladies' rest-room and before he'd been able to chicken out, the girls had started acting scary.

While May went to fetch some antiseptic lotion Mattie made for the bed and disappeared beneath the covers.

'Let's go,' said Rand, gamely.

'Are you okay?' asked May.

'Sure.' He mopped his white face. 'That ... hamster isn't going to stop me seeing New York.'

'Where *is* he?' asked Vera.

I began to hunt around the bed, with Vera shaking out the blankets. Mattie, cheeks stuffed full of food, was lying in a nest of his own making, built of May's blonde hair, feathers from the pillows and shreds of my waistcoat which he had stowed away on the journey from England. I picked up that slight, silky mischief-maker, put him in his cage and bolted it securely.

'I gotta have a little animal,' said May, as we walked out of the hotel. 'I need him in my work.'

'In a laboratory?' asked Rand.

'Why, not exactly ... I'm kinda on the human side.'

'Public relations?'

'I guess so ... There's some shopping I have to do ... also in connection with my work. Do you mind? In my job a girl needs the right kinda telephone.'

There were all kinds of telephones for sale in the Avenue of the Americas, besides foreign and native switchboards, tape-recorders, radios, transistors, things from levis, capri-pants, sandals called go-aheads, to *English West-end Mis-fits.*

George's, the shop into which May led us, appeared to be something of a misfit too. It was crammed full of the types of telephones I remembered seeing as a small boy in the Post Office or the doctor's surgery of North Scottish hamlets such as Meall Meadhonach.

'Our selection of antique telephones,' said the well-dressed elderly salesman, 'is the finest in the United States, ma'am. Name any model you wish. If it's not right here, we'll get it for you inside a month. Personally I'd recommend to you this 1891 gear-model ... or the Swedish model first manufactured by the best craftsmen in 1908.'

May picked up a complicated-looking receiver. 'I was thinking of a telephone you can fix on the wall. I got six-teenth-century eastern furniture in my ... office. A wall-phone would look kinda cute with it.'

'The 1893 Newton.' The salesman went to the back of the

shop and returned with a chipped, black instrument as clumsy as anything I'd seen in Meall Meadhonach. 'I wouldn't show this to another customer, ma'am; it looks just a piece of junk, doesn't it? Only a customer with imagination could figure out what it'll be like when our workshop's through renovating it ... We'll put a good solid gold-plating on all the metal parts and the enamel can be matched with the colour of your walls or your curtains. Then we fix the instrument with a dial, gold-plated of course, and rewire.'

'Pretty,' said an old lady, who had joined us. She was leaning on a stick, gazing at the telephone with a collector's attentiveness. 'But you haven't *bought* it, dear, have you?'

'Why, no,' said May, 'not yet.'

'*Don't* buy.' The old lady was so emphatic that her flower-petal hat slipped to her eyebrows, 'Antique telephones are a scourge ... a real scourge.' She opened her handbag and brought out a letter. 'You read *this*, honey.'

We all read it – a long letter from the New York Telephone Company, referring to its previous communications with the subscriber, Miss Eleanora Cabanocotti. The Company begged to inform the subscriber that her antique telephone had, once again, been the cause of creating a chaotic situation in a large sector of its nation-wide network. While making allowances for the personal tastes of individual subscribers, the Company felt it had become essential to safeguard the convenience of the majority of its customers. Should Miss Cabanocotti's instrument cause another breakdown in the Company's services, action would have to be taken.

'What action?' asked May.

'Court-action, I guess.' The old lady shrugged her shoulders. 'But the case they started five years ago hasn't been heard yet.'

'Then you're *selling* your telephone?' asked the salesman.

'Selling? No ... not at all. I want another instrument, preferably the same model. You remember? I bought a wall-telephone ... I believe it's the same as this one.'

May snatched the telephone from the salesman's hand. 'I'm taking it.'

'Well, well,' said the old lady, 'I warned you, honey.'

'But you want to buy one yourself.'

'I wouldn't, if I were your age. When you're young life is too short for litigation.' The flower-hat nodded towards the salesman, 'I'll visit with you again. Good day.'

'Do you still want this telephone?' asked Rand.

'Sure ... A friend of mine in Hollywood had his phone covered in fur. That's what I want.'

'Something soft, ma'am,' suggested the salesman. 'Like hamster?'

'Hamster!' May almost shouted. 'How cruel can you get!'

'Mink, ma'am?'

'Mink?' She ran her fingers over her coat. 'Yes, that would be real nice. But no gold-plating. It wouldn't look right with platinum mink. I'll have the metal parts in silver.'

Walking out of the shop I picked up one of George's business cards. But even with such proof in my possession I doubted whether I'd succeed in convincing my Julia that there *was* a place that sold gold- or silver-plated, mink-covered, antique telephones capable of disrupting 'a large sector of the nationwide network'.

I collected business cards and leaflets all over the Rockefeller Centre, but none of them entirely conveyed that amazing city within the city, the subterranean docks swallowing great convoys of trucks, the giant figures of Brangwyn's murals hovering above indoor streets crammed with shops selling anything from a fifty-thousand-pound diamond necklace to goldfish in plastic bags.

Here was the prototype of human-existence-in-the-future. Man *could* live permanently under cover, no longer exposed to crudities such as changeable skies, heat, cold, dryness or dampness.

The Rockefeller Centre was equipped for every contingency, a gymnasium or an ice-skating rink for the fat, delicatessen shops or the Rainbow Room restaurant or the Tower Suite cocktail bar on the 48th floor of the Time & Life Building for the thin. For the bored, the Radio City

Music Hall; for the lonely, a pup or a vitamin-raised kitten from the pet shop; doctors and drug-stores for the sick; for those who went off their heads, a choice of psychiatrists, alienists or analysts; for the dead a luxurious funeral-parlour, make-up artists and live music from a string-quartet; for the claustrophobic an observation tower, on the 70th floor, that spread New York at one's feet.

Here was the complete New Way of Life, and if one wanted to know how such a miracle had begun the explanation was on the spot: the Museum of the Chase Manhattan Bank. The raw material for under-cover living was displayed in tidy show-cases – 75,000 specimens of money from the earliest nugget to notes of Hitler Germany, coins commemorating the election of some Asian premier or celebrating a *coup d'état* in which an African politician had elected *himself* premier.

The more I saw of that miraculous indoor city the more kindly I remembered those filthy, raw English November mornings of trudging through muddy fields after some sick cow.

It was the goldfish in plastic bags that got us out in the open again. The goldfish reminded Rand that he had promised to call at the *Bide-A-Wee Association Inc.* on behalf of a client who wanted to join the Dogs' Pension Plan. Vera and May agreed; *Bide-A-Wee* was on 38th Street, not far from the Empire State Building which – they insisted – we had to see between sundown and night.

Bide-A-Wee looked like a back-street shop near any waterfront, the only distinguishing mark being a kind of coat-of-arms with the motto *Loyalty, Devotion, Forgiveness, Humour* and a *bas-relief* of three dogs almost rampant. Inside, there were rows of wire-gated kennels and photographs of dogs in the more luxurious surroundings of armchairs and embroidered cushions.

The girl who showed us round was friendly, matter-of-fact and faintly alarmed when obviously timorous dogs began to growl at the sight of Rand.

'Our procedure's simple,' she explained. 'Any dog over the age of five is eligible for our pension plan ... subject to a physical examination by a veterinarian, signing of a con-

tract and – of course – payment of the fees. We charge
three hundred dollars a year ... and we give easy payment
terms.' She gave each of us a leaflet advertising the ameni-
ties.

GOOD HOME FOR YOUR OLD PET.

200 acres in Suffolk County, Long Island,

Attractive kennel buildings,

Modern heating to maintain even temperatures for old
    dogs,

Spacious outdoor runs with plenty of sunshine and shade
    areas,

Medical treatment when necessary,

Trained kennelmen to care for your pet,

Nourishing foods and special diets for the older dog.

'I wouldn't mind being an older dog,' said Rand, gazing
at the photograph on the front cover which looked like
something out of *Country Life*. 'Two hundred acres ... I
guess one day there'll be places that good for old *people*.'

'You shouldn't say things like that,' whispered Vera. 'Do
you want people to take you for a *Red*?'

The *Bide-A-Wee* girl pointed to a couple of coloured
photographs above the door. 'You see, the grounds are
landscaped real pretty. And here's the visitor's room ... You
know, we also act as an Adoption Society. Here's a price-list
... it's a scale of *donations* really. We charge a little more
for spayed or altered pets. If you adopt an animal from us
you've got to sign a pledge ... just so we're sure you'll treat
it right ... Maybe you'd like to see some puppies. The
nursery ...'

'No, thanks.' Rand made for the door, herding us out in
front of him. 'It's a swell place, but it gives me – what did
you call it, Vera? – it gives me ... that psychological feeling.'

On the 102nd storey of the Empire State Building Vera's
feelings were less complicated than they had been at the
Guggenheim Gallery. With the floor stirring under us like
the deck of a ship, she leaned against my shoulder, well
aware that her warmth and the perfume of her hair was

28

sending shock-waves down my spine.

'Well, Michael?' she murmured.

I was meant to echo that 'well' with an equally soft sound. But I remembered Julia. 'Rather a fierce wind up here, isn't there?'

She did *not* remove her head from my shoulder. 'What do you think, Michael?'

'It's quite a building; though from the street it looks like an outsize hypodermic syringe.'

'The sunset...'

'Yes, that's something I've always noticed. Just before the sun goes down the details in a panorama are specially clear. I'm sure I counted eight liners at the Hudson River piers ... and I could pick out Grand Central Railway Station.'

'Railroad,' she corrected me, her voice still dreamy. 'Yes, but how about *now*?'

Now I was seeing one of the wonders of the world, New York blazing, flickering, gyrating in billions of lights. 'Looks nice,' I said; 'especially those brown-stone houses ... the slummier districts, I suppose. Like blocks of chocolate lit up from inside.'

'Chocolate!' She was beginning to sound annoyed. 'Have you got no imagination? You're in a building a quarter of a mile high; and the elevator took you up inside one minute. You can see as far as fifty miles...'

I was not going to be bullied by statistics into something Julia wouldn't like. 'I've *read* the leaflet,' I told Vera. 'We can see five States from here ... Let me see; Connecticut ... do you pronounce the second c or not? ... Massachusetts...' Vera's warmth was beginning to make my knees go weak. 'New Jersey ... Pennsylvania ... dash it, I can't remember the fifth State.'

'New York,' said Vera. It sounded more like 'darling'. 'You must be tired.'

'Never felt fresher in my life.'

'You haven't had anything to eat since lunch-time.'

'Can't say I'm hungry. But I dare say I'd manage a steak. Rand...' I grabbed him by the coat as he was trying to pass us on his umpteenth round of the observation terrace. 'Vera's hungry. Let's go and have dinner somewhere.'

'Sure,' said Rand. 'How about Rattazzi's on 48th Street? Guy I know gave me the address.'

'Or the House of Chan,' suggested May, coming out of the dark. 'A friend of mine in Hollywood always goes there when he's in New York. I get a kick outa Chinese food.'

'We don't have to go anywhere ... anywhere at all.' Vera jerked her head from under my nose. 'We can eat right here, in a cafeteria.'

CHAPTER THREE

In the morning it was Masters who put the coffee-tray beside my bed. Miss Vera and Mr Rand had gone out early, he told me; the Duchess was still resting and the Duke had an appointment with his medical adviser.

'Did Miss Vera leave a message for me?'

'No, sir.'

'How was she?' I asked, somewhat inanely.

'Now that you mention it, sir ... I did have the impression – nothing more definite than an impression, of course – that she was a little out of sorts.'

I too felt out of sorts after I'd phoned the Algonquin and learned that May and hamster had left for California. What could one do on one's own in New York? Photograph the sky-scrapers? Do the museums? Buy Julia an antique telephone? It seemed a good idea until it occurred to me that the Postmaster-General of England probably held greater powers over the instruments than any private telephone company. Besides, in England it did not take five years for a law case to be heard in court. The telephone was out.

I thought of New York as I'd seen it on the previous day, a land of glittering stalactites. And one of the most striking columns had been the United Nations Building. Seeing the UNO Building was the thing to do, especially for people from England who had money invested in that organization; whether soundly or not was too complicated a speculation at nine in the morning.

The taxi I hailed displayed a badge saying *In God I trust*, and as it bounded down Fifth Avenue I felt like answering back 'heaven help me'. But the driver got me to 48th Street without a dent.

I wandered along the East River, in the strong sun, working out the meaning of notice-boards – some professionally painted, some the work of amateur sign-writers: OUTEN

DOGS HERE, said one, BUTTON DON'T BELL, BUMP another; CAR
NO MORE, SIT DOWN ALONG HERE; TAKE A TIP FROM THE GLIS GLIS
OR FAT DORMOUSE – WHICH AS A PERMANENT SLEEPING-TREE –
REALTOR KUBITSHEK AT YOUR SERVICE; DIVORCE INVESTIGATIONS
ON CREDIT-TERMS; THINK OF THE OTHER GUY – DON'T WORSEN
THE LUSH-HOUR.

The variations of English I heard around the circular
information desk in the lobby of the UNO Building were
even more surrealist, ranging from the laziest American
drawl to Slavonic staccato: 'You people alvaiss gett stomack-
ache ... too much hygiene ... Now in my country the
pheasants eat mice ... what? Mice ... what you call corn on
the copp. So the stomack ...'

Those references to the human anatomy somehow stres-
sed the contrast between the vastness of the hall and the
fragility of the people who scurried about with brief-cases
under their arms. Men with stomachs had conceived and
built that great complex of halls and conference-rooms; and
men with stomachs were busying themselves in it, trying to
dismantle empires and dream up new ones. The money
spent on the *building*, I thought after a tour of the place,
had not been wasted. It would have made a splendid clinic
and operating-theatre for horses.

I browsed in the UNO bookshops, looked at the souvenirs
for sale in the German, Indian, French and Swedish shops,
bought a folio-sized postcard with a special UNO stamp for
Julia, and went into the coffee-bar to write it.

But there was a distraction, a small white poodle who
would not be ignored. When I overlooked his tail-wagging
and pawing he hunched his back and took an acrobatic leap
into my arms.

'Pip, down!' ordered his mistress. 'Get down at once!'

Pip was wearing a powder-blue outfit which covered his
front- and hind-legs as well as his back, and that garment
was embroidered with the initials D.A.F.

'We met at the Algonquin,' I reminded his owner.

'Oh yes, in the elevator.' Gay frowned. 'Down ... my
mother-in-law was being embarrassing about America.'

'Amusing ... about advertising and piped music.'

'I guess I worry too much ... Pip, stop licking Mr ...'

'Michael Morton,' I introduced myself.

To save Pip from the hiding he was about to receive I told Gay that I was a veterinary surgeon and therefore popular with intelligent animals. She believed me, allowing her poodle to regain his *sang-froid* in his own good time. I ordered more coffee, and gave up the intention of writing to Julia.

While Gay talked of her husband, a water-power expert temporarily attached to United Nations Headquarters, I studied her neat, narrow face, wondering whether it was capable of showing any emotion other than that determinedly mustered calm. Gay's face would have been appropriate to a cold or a sophisticated woman; I did not think she was either.

'... So we may have to go to Africa soon,' she was saying. 'And Clifford won't let me take more than three of my poodles.'

'You have excellent kennels in this country.'

'Not for well brought-up dogs. The D.A.F. has only one kennel-estate, though we're hoping to open another soon ... in California.'

'What is the D.A.F.?' I asked.

'Why, the *Decent Animals Federation*. You haven't heard of it? Sam Bagshot Junior ... our President, was interviewed on television only last night. Gus Baker was trying to be funny about our Federation, but Sam got out on top. Sam's a real inspiration to us.'

I told Gay I'd like to know about the work of Sam's organization. If it was setting up a training establishment for dogs in California the Duke and Duchess of Alanspring would probably change *their* plans and let me return to England.

'We're not interested in training animals,' she said. 'Our task is the training of owners.'

'Sounds sensible.'

'It is. If we're not savages it's our duty to make sure our animals become civilized at last ... There's a meeting of the D.A.F. New York Chapter this afternoon. I think I should take you along.'

*

Though the meeting of the *Decent Animals Federation*, New York Chapter, was taking place in an air-conditioned modern city office the tone of the meeting was somewhere between the biblical and the vaguely religious.

President Sam Bagshot's energetic voice was cataloguing dangers and iniquities. '... And if you consider an expenditure of one hundred thousand dollars high ... for much-needed re-education kennels in California, think of *one* fact, just one. In Los Angeles County alone there are 825,000 animals in *public* view without a stitch of clothes on them. Can you imagine how many auto-accidents were caused by such animals? By the driver being distracted by the nakedness of a horse or a dog? Why don't we take our children to strip-tease shows? Because such shows would be morally corrupting them. Yet we take the children to zoos and circuses where unclothed animals present *as* formidable a moral danger ... In the past year I've travelled 70,000 miles, addressing over two-hundred meetings. And if I have learned one thing it's this: the American public is ready to cure the paradox of *people* going about in clothes and *animals* naked. Thanks to our work thousands every day are re-evaluating their thinking. The growth of our Federation is the proof ... But let me sound a warning to the more extreme members of D.A.F. We *must* be realistic. It would be wrong to advocate clothing for animals which are not higher than four inches or longer than six. Nor can we expect cattle roaming isolated ranges to be put in clothes. All we can ask is that cats, dogs, cows, horses, mules, sheep and the like, which *are* in public view, should be decently covered in boxer shorts ... So far our experience has shown that animals *like* having clothes on, that they become more well-adjusted when covered. But, just as there are some nutty people who oppose our aims, so certain animals reject clothing. It is for such animals that we are opening the re-training kennels at Santa Monica ... As you will see from the balance-sheet you all received our funds now stand at 300,000 dollars. That's fine, just fine. But we mustn't be complacent. There's a constant drain on our resources. More than ever your Executive relies upon the generosity of individual members for our Federation's continuing growth and success.'

The audience of about fifty applauded and remained seated.

Sam Bagshot tossed down a glass of water, cleared his throat and began to sing *Fight the good fight*. Gay apologized to me for not joining in with the others; she was tone-deaf.

'You'd like to meet Sam Bagshot, wouldn't you?'

It would have been churlish to say no.

The moment the singing stopped she tucked Pip under her arm, took me by the sleeve and made for the platform. 'Sam, I want you to meet a friend of mine ... he's a veterinarian from England.'

Sam's welcome made me ashamed of my thoughts. I felt almost guilty when I had to admit that I did not know of any society in England with aims similar to the *Decent Animals Federation*'s. When he asked me whether I reckoned I might start a branch – or chapter – of the D.A.F. in London, I parried with a question which had preoccupied me throughout the meeting.

'Would you mind telling me ... If you clothe an animal does it know the difference?'

'Pardon me?'

'Between ...' I found his puzzled eyes disconcerting. 'Between boy and girl animals.'

'Well, I don't want to be personal, Mr Morton,' said Sam, 'but *you* go about dressed, don't you? Can *you* tell the ... hrrrm ... difference?'

I refrained from answering, and let Gay lead me away.

'You know something?' she put down Pip, who was pulling towards the exit. 'Sam's a doctor of philosophy.'

Pip had stopped at the first street-corner. Another question I had refrained from asking was about to be answered. Pip, lifting a leg, was able to carry out his intention unimpeded by his powder-blue garment.

'Stretch-nylon,' said Gay. 'The dogs need some new clothes. We could go order them right now.'

The BOUTIQUE was on the seventh floor of a new business block. The showroom had royal blue walls, a pale blue ceiling with mirror-glass stars and white leather armchairs. The leaflets scattered about mirror-topped tables advertised THIS YEAR'S FASHIONS FOR THE SMART LADY DOG and THE COMPLETE HOLIDAY WARDROBE FOR YOUR POODLE.

'I want to see models for a hot climate,' Gay told the tall, white-haired saleswoman. 'We're taking the dogs for a vacation in California. And afterwards we expect to live in Africa.'

'May I suggest the beach-fashions first, Mrs Petrell?'

'Yes, thank you, Miss Alberti.'

'Susie,' Miss Alberti said to a boy who had been waiting behind a leather-covered counter. 'Dress Susie in the Firenze and Dan in the Taft.'

Within a minute a curtain at the back of the showroom slid back revealing a black poodle of Pip's size, wearing a frilled white skirt, a short jacket embroidered with a red anchor and a white bonnet.

'Up, Susie!' said Miss Alberti.

Susie rose on her hind legs and began to turn like a human mannequin.

'Isn't her dress darling!' exclaimed Gay.

Her poodle didn't seem to think so. Pip had watched Susie's entrance with ears well up, interested to the point of straining at his lead, but when Susie had begun her mannequin act he'd looked baffled, embarrassed and finally disillusioned. He crept under the nearest chair and flattened himself, head well down on his paws.

The next mannequin was a white poodle, not unlike Pip, in a pair of white- and black-striped trousers reminiscent of Victorian bathing-trunks. Pip gave them one brief glance and yawned.

While we saw another twenty-odd models, from romping shorts to evening dresses, Gay made notes and Pip went to sleep. I found a price list; the dog-dainties cost anything from ten dollars to one hundred and fifty. Clearly Gay's bill for eight poodle-wardrobes was going to be as high as a wardrobe for herself, if not higher.

Miss Alberti had written down the order and promised to send the clothes by special messenger, when Susie came prancing back still dressed in a red evening-creation with a matching bow between the ears. Pip retreated behind his mistress, entangling Gay in the lead, but Susie followed.

They faced one another, Susie obviously annoyed by Pip's disdain, Pip embarrassed. He preserved his equanimity as long as he could stand it, but when Susie went sniffing around him he leaped forward and grabbed her bow. Susie kept growling and yapping long after Miss Alberti had picked her up, Pip continued savaging the red bow until Gay forcibly removed it.

'I don't know what's gotten into Pip,' said Gay, as we stepped into the lift.

I could have told her. But I didn't; she was looking worried and tired. 'Let's have a drink,' I suggested.

'Well, I'd like a Coca-Cola.'

We were standing on Fifth Avenue, with people streaming out of shops and offices, traffic nose to tail. All the taxis were full and – as in the London rush-hour – I wondered how their *occupants* had managed to hire them. Surely there was one of those nasty social injustices behind it.

'Hopeless,' said Gay.

'We could go to the Algonquin.'

'Or the club where I'm meeting my mother-in-law. It's only a few blocks along.'

Broadway was not far but it took us a long time to get through. The sidewalks were packed with people strolling along, posing for street-photographers or window-shopping. I did notice the names of a few well-known movie palaces, yet the most prominent feature of this theatre-land was the small transistor.

German, Japanese, Dutch and Empire transistor wireless sets packed the windows of most stores; no two stores put the same price on the same set, but all prices were marked up in blazing luminous paints. Gay said those emporiums were called discount-stores, meaning that they sold their wares cheaper than ordinary shops and kept up cut-throat competition among themselves. Just business; niceness in business had been a cute English idea which had gone out with President Lincoln's assassination.

'And that wasn't a nice thing to do either,' she said,

'shooting the President inside a *theatre*.'

'Killing heads of state at the opera used to be a Russian method.'

'Well, I might have known it ... You just can't trust the Russians.' She turned into a wood-panelled vestibule. 'No elevator to the second floor.'

On the first floor we came upon a large gold and black business plate: PETER SABINUS (ROME INC.) PROFESSOR OF ELOQUENCE. OFFICES ONE FLOOR UP.

Waiting for the lift outside the professor's offices we heard voices, apparently raised in agitation, 'Till *Lionel's* issue fails...'

'That just won't do, Mr Harris,' said a crisp executive baritone.

'Till Lionel's *issue* fails...'

'It will, Mr Harris, if you don't prodooce more confidence.'

'Lionel's!' exclaimed Gay. 'Did you hear what he said about their issue? My first husband left me shares in Lionel's. I'd better call my broker ... Listen!'

'Till Lionel's issue *fails*,' the first voice repeated more firmly, 'his should not reign. It fails not yet, but flourishes in thee ... And in thy sons ...'

'Shakespeare,' I suggested, opening the lift doors for Gay.

'Shakespeare? Are you positive?'

'I'm sure they weren't talking stocks and shares.'

'I guess there *is* a Lionel in Shakespeare?'

'Henry the Sixth, I believe.'

'Oh, well ... They had me worried. People shouldn't shout about issues. It isn't decent.' The lift rattled to top-floor level. Gay tucked Pip under her arm, and made for a scarlet-curtained doorway.

THE CLUB, I was glad to see, had nothing to do with clothed or with naked animals – only with stage-people. At the bar they perched in a long row like swallows on a tele-graph-wire; the rest of the club-members, still wearing grease-paint or stage-costume occupied tables separated from one another by outsize sandwich-boards advertising movies and Broadway-productions. These nesting-box-like arrangements did not allow space for long legs or visiting poodles.

'It looks run-down,' observed Gay, 'but THE CLUB is real old. I guess that's why my mother-in-law likes it. She's one of the founder-members. She told me it started up fifty years ago, the day she opened in her first show on Broadway.'

There had been a few innovations since then, most obvious of them the juke-boxes. Each table was fitted with its individual mini-juke-box, the collective noise of these little automats producing a sound similar to the bumbling of ill-tempered hornets in search of a home. The menu too had undoubtedly altered since the invention of the infra-red grill. The list on our table offered hot dogs, dachshunds, pups, corgis, wolves and great danes.

'It's a self-service,' said Gay.

'What would you like?'

'Coca-Cola, please.'

'How about a martini?'

'No, thanks, Michael. I don't like alcohol. But you go right ahead – if you don't care for Coca-Cola.'

'Well, I prefer something with a bit more body.'

Gay looked shocked, but almost at once her expression changed to friendly understanding. 'Sure, what you want is a milk-shake. They make them real well here.'

The milk-shake seemed the most popular drink among the club-members. While I waited for mine gallons of milk were being poured into machines, swirled about, pumped full of air and dispensed in unrecognizable consistencies.

My strawberry-shake certainly was a drink with body, so much body that no amount of sucking would draw it out of the tumbler. Gay listened sympathetically to the noises the milk-shake and I produced, and eventually went to find me a spoon.

While I chewed the stuff, wondering how much saliva one had to produce to get it past one's gullet, Dawn Petrell made an entrance. Surrounded by a retinue of Claire and Tiger, Vera and Rand, she greeted actors and actresses who recognized her, stopped for a word with the old Negro who was collecting used crockery, and acknowledged Pip's tail-wagging.

'It was fascinating, absolutely amazing,' she told Gay, accepting my seat.

'The dress-rehearsal of Tiger's play,' Vera told me. 'What happened to you? Didn't you want to see it?'

'You didn't ask me to.'

'Well, I kept calling you. Masters said you were out.' Vera appeared to have forgotten her annoyance with me. '*You* missed something ... Rand was swell.'

'Rand?'

'Sure. When those hippies started throwing things...'

'They weren't hippies, Vera,' said Rand.

'He just sprinted down after them,' Vera continued. 'And ...'

'I wasn't doing a thing,' Rand interrupted. 'I was just buying candies and those guys happened to pass.'

Their passing seemed to have done something to Rand's face. Apart from the scratch on the cheek, which he had acquired during his pursuit of May's hamster, his upper lip was swollen and there was a blood-clot adhering to his chin.

The taxis were still occupied, dashing down Broadway impervious to signalling pedestrians.

'As bad as London,' murmured Dawn, the grand old lady of the English stage. She removed her gloves, put two fingers of each hand in her mouth and produced a whistle that must have been heard throughout theatre-land.

Almost at once a taxi rolled up at her feet. 'No room for seven, ma'am,' the driver apologized.

'Well, then, we'll have another car. Please wait.' Dawn repeated her performance, this time attracting the attention of a driver who was being paid off on the opposite side of the street.

She gave an address at Long Island City, and watched while Gay, Rand and Vera got into the second car. 'Driver, better stop at a convenient wine-merchant's on the way.' Our taxi jumped into the traffic: 'Or a drug-store where they sell wines ... Gay's quite domesticated, but one can't be sure that she's equipped for cocktail-visitors. Of course Clifford will change all that, but they haven't been married very long ... Such an ordeal, a dress-rehearsal. You two children must be longing for refreshments.'

Claire sighed. 'A Bloody Mary will be wonderful.'

'You and Tiger used to drink Coca-Cola,' I said.

'We still do, Michael. But Tiger's discovered Bloody Mary ... we have it on special occasions. And today's one of them. Tiger, do tell Michael about the new dimension ... It was terribly exciting.'

'Well, yes,' agreed Tiger. 'You remember the play, don't you, Michael? Sometimes an actor does add a new dimension, even to a scene which is good to begin with.'

I heard Dawn Petrell beside me give a faint snort.

'Now,' Tiger's voice deepened to a true bass. 'This is what happened...' his voice droned on until Claire broke in: 'Isn't it absolutely glorious?'

Fortunately, knowing Claire, I realized it was a rhetorical question. 'Tell me, what happened to Rand Hegel?' I asked.

'Oh, it was nothing,' said Tiger. 'Some hooligans started throwing things at the actors ... rotten tomatoes. Don't know who let them in.'

'Darling,' Claire put her hand on Tiger's arm, 'I know you don't worry about that kind of thing. But I didn't like it a bit.'

'Neither did I,' said Dawn Petrell. 'Especially when that nice young veterinary surgeon was almost knocked out ... Poor ... what *is* the name of your twin-brother?' she asked me.

'Rand ... Bertrand Hegel. But we met only a couple of days ago.'

'You're not brothers?'

'No, we're not related.'

'Extraordinary! Still ... come to think of it, you do get these phenomena in nature. Two of Gay's poodles are identical too ... yet they come from breeders a thousand miles apart.'

There was no trace of poodles when Gay's husband let us into the apartment. Holding Gay's arm with one hand, Clifford shook hands with us and hustled us into what appeared to be a breakfast-room, a very small one.

41

'Oh no, honey,' objected Gay. 'We don't want to be in here. The drawing-room is...'

'Leave it to me, darling.' Clifford flung open a cupboard, displaying an array of bottles. 'Everything's organized.' He caught her by the shoulders, stopping her from opening the door at the back of the room. 'Happy birthday, darling.' He dexterously swivelled her into an embrace.

'But, Clifford ... you wished me happy birthday in the morning. Don't you remember? You gave me this beautiful bracelet and...'

'And now I've made you a special fruit cocktail ... No, nothing alcoholic ... Come on, mother, pour it out; you do it so beautifully, long practice I suppose. And the cocktail-shaker's full of martini.'

Dawn accepting that her son had no intention of taking his hands off his wife, smiled and dispensed the drinks. We wished Gay many happy returns, and Gay said her fruit cocktail was delicious. Clifford launched into a detailed explanation of how it was made, beginning with a description of the supermarket where he had bought the oranges, the small shop where he'd found greengages and the drug-store which specialized in canned Hongkong lichi.

The ingredients accounted for, he told us how he had chopped, squashed, squeezed and generally mutilated them. Only a new wife in love could have listened so attentively. Dawn watched her son with concern, Claire suppressed yawns, Tiger was playing havoc with his ginger beard, Vera and Rand were holding a whispered conversation behind my back, and I considered pouring myself another martini.

'The telephone,' said Gay, disengaging herself.

'I'll take it.' Clifford, almost knocking down his mother, failed to reach the door before Gay.

'Oh!' The cry of horror made us rush after her. Gay was lying on the floor, an apparently lifeless poodle in her arms. Worse, six other small poodles lay strewn all over the drawing-room, deaf to the names Gay was calling out, oblivious of the telephone-bell.

'Darling,' Clifford kneeled down beside her. 'It's all right, darling ... it's all right. It was your birthday...'

'My birthday!' screamed Gay. 'My birthday! You ...

you! ...'

'Hang on, dear ... Listen, Gay, it was the telephone. The *telephone*, Gay. Don't you see? There's nothing wrong with the dogs. They're just tired out.'

'They're sick,' sobbed Gay. 'That's why you wouldn't let us come in here. Oh, *do* something.'

'Yes,' said Rand, 'we'd better look at them.' He bent down and began examining the nearest animal, Pip's double. For once he was perfectly safe; the dog was completely limp and unresisting. So were the other dogs we examined. We could find nothing wrong with them other than signs of exhaustion; all they needed was rest and sleep, and that's what *they* had prescribed for themselves.

'How did you get them *that* tired?' asked Rand.

Clifford straightened up, drawing Gay to her feet. 'I found them like this when I got home ... You see, before we got married Gay had a job; she didn't have time to exercise the dogs ... well, not enough. So she trained them to run about the apartment when the telephone-bell rings ... of course, only when she's out.'

'You mean, you call your dogs on the telephone?'

'Yes.' Gay wiped her eyes. 'I let it ring for an hour ... It's kept them real fit ... until ...'

'It was your birthday,' said Clifford. 'I'm certain. People know you're not at the office any more so they rang up to give you their good wishes.'

Gay looked at the impervious bodies at her feet. 'Gee, I never knew I had so many friends.'

'There's nothing to worry about,' Rand assured her. 'Just let them sleep it off.'

'Let's have a drink,' said Clifford, returning to the break-fast-room.

Dawn, relieved that marriage had *not* turned her son into a bore, began to chatter about Tiger's peculiar dramatic talent; Claire described to me the happenings at the dress-rehearsal. It was so unusual for her to miss any remark about her husband's plays that I realized how much the afternoon's hooliganism still bothered her.

'Rand's right,' she told me. 'The men who threw the tomatoes ... *and* eggs ... at the stage, *weren't* hippies. They

43

looked more like ... businessmen, I suppose. If they do it on our first night ... Oh, Michael, it would be too dreadful.'

'Any way of finding out who they are?'

'We *know*.'

'You do?'

'Well, they presented Tiger with a sort of petition before the dress-rehearsal ... a perfectly ridiculous ultimatum signed by ... oh, about thirty people. So, you see, even if the men who came today are kept out on first night there are others who might make trouble. It's too bad of them ... asking Tiger to take three whole lines out of his play. It's ... it's victimization. Of course Tiger won't change a word.'

CHAPTER FOUR

'Willard!' The Duchess, sweeping into the room among her leaping terriers, halted in front of her husband's chair. 'I thought you *liked* Claire and Tiger!'

'Course I do. Charming girl, Claire. Very good with animals ... especially greyhounds. Most sympathetic when Grey Rainbow was off colour. You know, Sonia, something's just occurred to me; that cat, Chou-en-Lai, Claire always wears round her neck ... well, if you ask *me*, she wouldn't be keeping cats at all if Tiger didn't make her gallivant from pillar to post. If that husband of hers let her settle down ... say, at Craftly, she'd be keeping dogs instead.'

'Willard.' The Duchess sounded reproachful. 'Honey, you *can't* go to Tiger's first night in these cord-trousers.'

'Well ... er, I thought maybe I won't go. You go, dear. You've got Rand, Vera and Michael. I mean, even numbers and all that.'

'Claire would be real hurt if you're not there.'

'But I went to the opening of *Three Brassieres to Bond Street*, Sonia.'

'Why, yes, but that was Tiger's *first* play.'

'Second's much the same.'

'Oh, it isn't,' objected Vera, putting down the latest copy of *Harper's Bazaar*. 'Mother's right. You can't just chicken out of it tonight. Claire and Tiger are *your* friends.'

The Duke slowly unfolded himself and got up. 'When I met the two of them they were perfectly normal, healthy youngsters ... How was *I* to know that Tiger had this thing about writing plays?'

'I didn't trim Tiger's beard very well.' Claire nervously shifted Chou-en-Lai from her left shoulder to her right.

'Looks all right to me,' said the Duke, making room for a white fox-coat with a small woman inside. The foyer of the theatre was bulging with big furs, slim women and well-

45

shaven men. 'Queer lot, these fellows.' The Duke scrutinized the crowd besieging Tiger. 'No wonder he looks
browned-off.'

'Willard!' the Duchess pleaded, 'Honey, there are words
you use in all innocence ... I guess ... which no gentleman
can say out loud in the States. Queer's bad ... but *browned-
off*; well, that's terrible.'

'Why?'

'It's an army expression.'

'I know, Sonia.'

'It isn't one you can use *here*.'

'Perfectly all right in England. Don't worry, dear. Try not
to disgrace you.'

'Corcorran O'Tool,' Claire whispered. '*He's* the most important one.'

'Of what?' asked Rand.

'The *critic* O'Tool.' Claire glanced at me, apparently de-
ciding that there *were* people who had never heard of
Corcorran O'Tool.

'Mr St George Clemens,' the little critic shouted across his
colleagues, 'there's been an interesting rumour that you've
introdooced a noo dimension in the play.'

Tiger ploughed his way towards him. 'That's right. One
of those lucky accidents. The credit should really go to
Dave ... fellow who plays Jack.'

'Kitchen-sink stuff, I guess,' said a critic, behind me.

'No, anti-play drama,' corrected his companion.

'For crying out loud! What's the point?'

'Don't think it's *got* one. You're a square, Bill. You wanta
read that book by ... *You* know the one I mean. Written by
the professor at Harvard; or was it Oklahoma? It's this
theory about writing plays without words ... the dramatist
says nothing significant because he reckons words have lost
their meaning ... what with politicians using them up the
way they do.'

'Great! Then what are we here for? I can write my stuff
where I can get a drink.'

'Hi ... wait for baby!'

Suspense. The audience had noticed that the curtain had

46

risen and was waiting for the stage to light up. It didn't. After a while my eyes became adjusted to the darkness, and besides memory came to my assistance. Hadn't Claire read me the beginning of the play? So there it was; a lot of vapour – no doubt representing fog in Wandsworth – the dim outlines of a bicycle-shed, a kind of lean-to and a disused gas-cooker. An almost invisible figure appeared to be working a pump trying to inflate a bicycle-tyre. I thought somebody might have taken the trouble to oil that pump; but perhaps it was *meant* to sound tortured. After five minutes or more I became convinced that the pump's screeching was meant to torture the *audience*.

There was an angry growl somewhere in the stalls. Then came the sounds of objects dropping on to the stage, softish objects like over-ripe fruit.

'Trouble?' asked Rand.

'Seems like it,' agreed Vera.

By this time there were yells of rage in the circle as well as in the stalls. Missiles began to fly indiscriminately. No doubt the objectors were bent on intimidating the audience as well as cast and author. Something squashy bounced off Rand's head and splashed my hands. Judging by certain noises both the Duchess and Vera had been hit.

'That's enough.' The Duke got up. 'We're leaving, Sonia.' 'But honey...'

'Sonia, this is something you'd better leave to me. They're rotten shots, but I won't risk your getting hurt. Out!'

A few other people shared the Duke's opinion, among them Dawn Petrell. We met her at the nearest exit.

'How nice,' she greeted Rand and myself. 'You were most kind the other evening. Gay's writing to you. I can't imagine *what* would have happened without veterinary surgeons on the spot. Her poodles did look rather dead, didn't they?'

Naturally Dawn had met the Duke in England, and the Duchess had – of course – seen Dawn in some wonderful plays ... Bernard Shaw's or Ivor Novello's ... anyway nothing as worrying as Tiger St George Clemens's drama.

'Worrying indeed,' said Dawn. 'I lay awake all night wondering what the dear young man actually *means* ... Do

47

let's have a drink ... My club is just across the road ... Forgive me,' she produced a little embroidered handkerchief, and dabbed at Rand's face. 'Tomato, I suppose. I hope it didn't aggravate the bruise on your chin ... Well, we're looking fairly unscathed. Let's go.'

At the entrance to THE CLUB a group of girls, in the starlet uniform of brief skirts and beehives, were gossiping about 'Tiger's first night'. On the second floor, in his office beside the lift, the Professor of Eloquence was working late.

'No, no, Mr Schnabel,' he was protesting. 'Your double-u still has that aggressive ring ... It might give your stoodents the impression that you're suffering from an inferiority complex. Let's hear these lines again.'

'One of the prettiest touches of all,' began Mr Schnabel, 'and that vich ... which ... angled for mine eyes, caught the vater though not the fish ...'

'Fish!' Dawn Petrell frowned. 'The last thing one wants to hear just now ... I do hope this isn't the office of the *Friends of the Fish Society*.'

'... Caught the water, though not the fish ...' Mr Schnabel repeated, doggedly, 'vas, ven ... was, ven, was when ... at the relation ...'

'Ah, Shakespeare,' said Dawn. 'We're safe.'

'Not Henry the Sixth?' I asked.

'No, no ... The Winter's Tale. Third Gent speaking, if I remember rightly. It's a long time since I did my stint of Shakespeare.'

'The lift seemed to run more smoothly than on my previous ride to THE CLUB, and when it stopped I noticed that the scarlet curtain had been replaced by a transparent plastic screen which folded back concertina fashion.

It folded back, revealing an entirely transformed place. What had been shabby was now gaudy. The sandwich-boards had been replaced by screens with Jackson Pollock designs; the individual juke-boxes had given way to one great machine whose noise was far more pervading than the humming of the miniature automats. There were patterns everywhere – palm-trees on curtains, ships on walls, surrealist flower-pots on chairs. No two walls or windows were covered with the same material or design. What had been wood was now anodized metal, even the bar.

'What is the meaning of this?' Dawn asked the old Negro waiter, who was wearing a new striped cotton-suit with a red bow-tie.

'They come in yesterday and make everything new, ma'am.'

'You should have warned me, Sammy.'

'I didn't know,' the Negro shrugged his shoulders. 'Nobody know. You like it, ma'am?'

'It's ... restless.'

When Sammy had gone to fetch our highballs Dawn apologized for bringing us to such a place. 'Someone,' she said, 'and I mean to find out who, has indulged a frenzy of good taste ... or rather, just *taste*.'

'Not too bad.' The Duke ran his fingers along the dull-gold metal edge of our table. 'A bit jazzy, I dare say, but all right as these modern places go.'

'Willard's amazing,' the Duchess told Dawn. 'He has a real feeling for our American way of life; he adjusts better than I do.'

'Well, Mother, you are a slow adjuster,' said Vera. 'Dr Bonblust *told* you you're alienated.'

'Aren't we all?' asked Rand. 'I read an article by Professor Carson; he says we're not persons any longer. We're statistics, and if a statistical figure behaves like an individual then he upsets the other statistical figures. So ... if you *are* an individual you're a nuisance and nobody wants you. So you get kinda lonesome. I suppose that's what alienated means.'

'Rubbish!' The Duke patted his wife's hand. 'Sonia's got nothing to do with statistics ... or alienation, or I wouldn't have married her. Perfectly normal woman. Nothing the matter with this club either.'

'I don't know,' Vera gazed at Rand. 'This place gives me a psychological feeling. *You* know.'

Rand nodded. 'It sure does. I guess Tiger sees things that way ... You think of his stage-set in the first act. If Tiger had been raised in the States he couldn't have gotten across better ...'

*

The newspapers we read at breakfast differed considerably in their views on *what* Tiger's play had meant to get across. The *New York Times* described *Three Corsets to Curzon Street* as a serious work by an English intellectual which almost succeeds in stating a central problem of our age but falls into the trap of over-dramatization.

The drama-critic of the *Post* felt the play foundered in the quicksands of imperialism, traditional stumbling-block of the English artist.

The *News* said Mr St George Clemens was a most unEnglish dramatist whose spiritual home was, quite obviously France. The play was imbued with a deplorable French chauvinism.

The *Review* congratulated Tiger on a charming comedy of manners, and condemned the hooliganism of a section of the first-night audience.

The *Clarion* hailed the play as a brilliant experiment in modern theatre and congratulated Tiger on achieving slightly perilous but 'committed' audience-participation.

The play was launched and labelled; Claire and Tiger no longer needed my moral support – or rather, they no longer provided me with an excuse for savouring New York. A well-timed letter from Julia, propped up against my coffee cup, reminded me that I was not on holiday. My fiancée had approved my 'wasting a few days' for the sake of seeing Tiger's play, but now she wanted to know when I was going to California and how long it would take me to organize the Duchess's *Wee Souls' Sanctuary Inc.* There was a postscript with more than one meaning: 'Don't forget to write the day of your return. Tell about the animals you're seeing ... I suppose you *are* seeing animals as well as people. You don't want me to return the wedding presents we received prematurely, or do you?'

'You're looking worried,' said Vera, buttering her toast.

'I have ... obligations in England,' I told her. 'I should go to California as soon as possible.'

'Don't see why not.' The Duke put down his paper. 'What are we waiting for, Sonia?'

'We *were* waiting for the results of your medical checkup, Willard.'

'Didn't we get it a couple of days ago?'

'Sure.'

'It's okay, isn't it?' asked Vera.

'Why, of course.'

'So we can go,' suggested Rand. '*I* should be getting back to California.'

The Duchess opened a small leather-bound diary which had been lying beside her plate. 'I guess our veterinary surgeons could go ahead; what do you think, Willard? They might do the preliminary work. *We* can't leave New York just yet.'

'Can't we?'

'You have to see your tailor next week.'

'Tailors in Santa Monica, I dare say.'

'Honey, there's only *one* Gluckstein.'

'Yes,' muttered the Duke, 'and he's getting too big for my boots.'

'That tuxedo he made for you...'

The sartorial argument was likely to continue until the dogs demanded their walk. I excused myself from the table, saying I'd book my flight to California right away.

Vera followed me into the lounge. 'You don't have to book, Michael. We can just take a taxi to La Guardia airport and catch the next plane.'

'We?'

'Oh, haven't I told you? We're flying to Nevada because Rand left his car in Reno. We'll pick it up and drive to California.'

'The *three* of us?'

'Yes.' My caution seemed to annoy her.

'How far is it by road?'

'Two days ... With Rand about I'm not likely to go mad gambling in Reno, am I? So we won't waste your time.'

'Wouldn't you rather go with Rand? I mean I could fly directly...'

'I would *not* rather go with Rand,' she mimicked me. 'A twosome with Rand would land me on the flight-deck.'

'Where?'

'An institution for mental cases.'

'I thought you and Rand...'

'*Don't* think,' said Vera, sweetly. 'How do you know thinking isn't an un-American activity?'

Between our arrival at the airport and buying the tickets Vera's mood improved. And when she heard that our jet would leave an hour late she was delighted. What could be better? Now she had time to show me round, and Rand could buy us drinks: root-beer, a traditional American beverage, was something to which a foreigner *should* be introduced.

There was a familiar taste to the root-beer, a revolting taste I could not immediately identify. But as the flavour persisted in my mouth I remembered the smell of the ointment my grandfather had used against rheumatic twinges. Wintergreen. I wandered off, glass in hand, looking for some place to get rid of the stuff. I considered trashcans, which were unfortunately perforated, rubber-plants – all of them too high up or too public – and slot-machines. On the whole the slot-machines were the most promising receptacles, but a touch of social conscience made me hesitate in case the root-beer gummed up the works. I felt the least I could do was to check the purpose of the automats; a man could do without that extra packet of cigarettes but a milk-machine might be vital to a baby.

One particularly elaborate automat forced my thoughts upon my imminent journey. It displayed a man about to board a plane, waving to a bunch of smiling children. *Insure their future*, said a caption underneath. Though my children were still unborn there was no getting away from the fact that I had made a first move by almost marrying Julia. I imagined how touched Julia would be if the plane crashed, if I were killed and she received five thousand dollars insurance money. *That* would prove to her at last how faithful I'd been.

I put in the requisite number of coins. There was some chugging and gurgling inside the machine, and presently my policy came sliding out. I was about to leave, the root-beer still with me, when the automat gave a sharp click. I looked back, in case it had decided to give me a discount; instead a voice came crooning from one of the slots, 'Are

52

you sure it's enough?'

For a moment I felt pretty mean. Julia surely deserved more than five thousand dollars compensation for the loss of my devotion.

'Are you sure it's enough?' repeated the automat, on a fading note.

Five thousand dollars was not a fortune. But Julia wouldn't expect to make capital out of my demise. On the other hand she had her moments of shrewdness; the threat of returning our wedding-presents had been one of them.

'Are you sure,' gasped the dying voice from the automat, 'it's enough?'

'Yes, thanks,' I said, putting the plastic beaker of root-beer on top of the machine.

Vera and Rand had been looking for me. 'Hurry up, Michael! We're going to miss the plane. Where have you been?'

'I've bought an insurance policy.'

'No!' Vera sounded appalled.

'Does it give you that psychological feeling?'

'Sure,' she answered me, quite seriously.

'I've never yet collected on an insurance policy,' I tried to comfort Vera, as we boarded the plane.

'*Madre de Diós*,' prayed a young Mexican mother in the seat behind me. '*Dejadlo al villano pene; véngueme Diós delle* ... Let the wretch be punished; may God avenge me on him.'

53

CHAPTER FIVE

In the air above Chicago the Mexican mother was still asking God to punish someone by the name of Sean. Her two small boys went their independent ways; the one with *Micky Finn* written across his T-shirt kept patrolling the plane, gun in hand, boots creaking so loudly that I soon thought of nothing but boots and why they creaked; the other boy, with *Huckleberry Hound* on his shirt stationed himself at the lavatory door, which he opened and closed on request.

Above Denver it suddenly occurred to the mother to ask me whether I came from England. She was so pleased to have guessed my nationality that she asked Rand to change places with her and came to sit beside me. As an Englishman, she told me, I had something in common with her sons – Sean, their father, came from Dublin. It had been her rotten luck to marry a wild drunken Dubliner when she *could* have married a proper London Englishman.

She'd come to her senses at last. Though she'd always be sad about upsetting her priest she'd go through with it – she was going to Reno to divorce her husband. Perhaps God would hear her prayers; her church was against divorce, so maybe God would help her in her dilemma and make Sean drop dead. If God *didn't* listen to her she'd go to confession the day after the divorce. It wasn't as if she hadn't explained to Him the snags of living with a man who got drunk and threw away his money on horse-betting.

The creaking boots of Micky Finn accompanied the mother's harsh voice; Huckleberry Hound banged the lavatory door; and Vera kept glancing up from her hefty novel, apparently trying to assess whether I was enjoying the Mexican woman's company.

By the time we landed Vera was convinced that *I* had struck up a friendship with the Mexican, and showed her displeasure by ignoring my presence in the taxi. I tried to see things her way. What *was* a girl to think of a man who

54

deliberately missed a romantic opportunity on top of the most romantic skyscraper in the world and then spent hours in the air being attentive to an attractive stranger? There was nothing for it; if I did not convince Vera that I hadn't meant to slight her the rest of our journey would be miserable.

As the taxi stopped outside the Golden Hotel I gave Vera's waist a hug, and picked up her luggage before Rand could display his manners.

She was not impressed. 'What would you like to do, Rand?' she asked.

'I guess I'll call my mother and tell her I'm picking up the car ... Or maybe not. She'd want us to have dinner with her...'

'Well, why not?'

'It's kinda quiet at her place. You wouldn't like it. Let's show Michael the town ... I'll go get the car in the morning. Okay?' He didn't wait for an answer, making a dive for the lift. 'Meet you down here in half an hour.'

I spent the best part of the half-hour securing a bellboy, explaining that I wanted him to buy a spray of orchids for the lady in Room 246 and exploring my own room. In the bathroom I found shoeshine tissues, razor tissues, face tissues, a bottle-opener and a corkscrew; the bedroom was equipped with a dozen pink-tinted mirrors, a ticket for a drink on the house, and a one-armed bandit which took ten cents a time.

Waiting for Vera and Rand I realized that the Golden Hotel's furniture consisted chiefly of one-armed bandits, fruit-machines, roulette-tables, crap and blackjack tables. There were lobbies full of them, gaming halls and bars. The smallest public room had a circular bar with bottles and barmen in the centre and the customers perched on stools on the circumference. In front of every stool there was a lever – not a gadget for filling your own beerglass – but a sunk-in one-armed bandit. The customers didn't have to take the trouble of putting their change in their pockets; it was simpler to let the one-armed bandit have it.

Rand joined me at the bar. He too had received a ticket

for a complimentary drink. 'Tried the machines yet?'

I said I hadn't.

'Well, I shouldn't if I were you.' He mournfully watched an elderly lady feed one of the fruit-machines. 'My mother's lost a fortune in the supermarkets ... they've got machines in the stores too ... for the housewife who *wouldn't* come in here. Mother doesn't approve of bars.' He gazed at Vera, who had made an entrance in a delightful lilac-coloured silk-suit. 'Mother doesn't approve of young girls either ... I guess *everything* I like's either immoral, fattening or forbidden.'

'What's forbidden, Rand?' asked Vera, draping herself on the stool beside me.

'*Everything* in Reno ... when I lived here.'

'Poor Rand.'

'I dunno. Anyway who wants to play the machines?'

'Are the orchids from you, Michael?' Vera touched her spray, which looked just right against the pale silk.

'Like them?'

'You're swell.' Her hair touched my face. 'For crying out loud!'

Rand almost fell off the stool at the sight which had startled Vera, and I – already overwhelmed by the rattling of so many fruit-machines – wondered whether one glass of bourbon on the rocks could have given us hallucinations. I kept staring at the party which was making for our bar, but my first impression refused to alter.

What we saw were about ten women between the ages of sixty and eighty, some dressed in scarlet satin pyjamas heavily encrusted with sequins, others wearing orange-coloured transparent trousers – full but gathered at the ankles – gold boleros and great green turbans topped with ostrich-feathers, or – even more amazing – Ophelia-like floating garments in white with coronets of silver-beaded flowers.

They marched, waddled and limped up to the bar; the most committee-chairmanlike of them ordered Pepsi-Cola, and put a nickel into the nearest fruit-machine. There were clicks, sounds of dropping coins and squeals of pleasure. 'Why, Violet! You're a lucky one, and that's the truth.'

The ladies' laughter rattled the glasses on the bar.

'Go ahead, Amy ... *You* try.'

'Did you hear what Peachy said?' croaked the oldest of the Ophelias. 'Truth, she said ... *truth*.'

There was another gust of laughter, syncopated by the clicking of the machines.

Rand's face was looking pinched. 'Let's get outa here.'

'They're cute,' said Vera, doubtfully. 'Do you know some place we can eat?'

'Sure.' Rand took her by the arm. 'Come on ... There *must* be places ...'

There were. But every restaurant we looked into was crowded with Ophelias, houris and scarlet-pyjamaed cowboys over sixty. Some of the establishments had draped their entrances with banners, *Reno welcomes the Sisters of the Tibetan Truth*. The Sisters appeared to have taken over all of Reno, and I wondered where the town had tucked away its more ordinary visitors and citizens.

'We'd better go to my mother's,' said Rand, dejectedly.

'No.' Vera stood her ground in the foyer of a restaurant with fountains and plastic palm-trees. 'I think the *Sisters of the Tibetan Truth* are cute, real cute.'

'They send me up the flight-deck.' Rand's retreat was cut off by the entrance of a couple of houris. 'Michael, have you ever seen a more depressing sight? Thousands of old ladies in fancy-dress ... holding a congress, I guess. Just look at their faces. Ever seen anything more discontented? Anything harder?'

'Crap,' said Vera.

'No, it isn't. That's the American female for you. It starts at college, with the petting. You pet a girl a shade more than you should, and the next thing you know you're married. Then it's either divorce and a big alimony to pay the rest of your life or you get along in a fashion ... usually her fashion. If she's a girl with a profession you'll kill yourself doing her house-work ... that's the equality-racket. If she stays at home she'll soon let you know what she'd be earning if she weren't tied down. For the sake of peace you get earning as hard as you can, and you'll drop dead with a heart-attack at a ripe young age. But if you survive, and you can afford it, you go in for a boy's life ... committees, politics, fraternities. So you get lonesome, dissatisfied girls who start women's societies to replace the thing they've ruined for themselves.'

Vera applauded, 'Why, Rand, that was quite a speech.' A waiter, mistaking the clapping for impatience, came hurrying across the restaurant.

'Three, ma'am?' The waiter offered us a table beside a large group of houris.

'Thank you.' Vera gave him a sweet smile, and sat down. 'What *you* need, Rand, is a big he-man steak ... then, maybe, you'll feel less scared of girls.'

Our dinner would have been a constrained affair if we hadn't been so busy listening to the Ophelias at the next table. I, for one, wanted to know what had induced so many old ladies to shed all inhibitions and wander around in transparent harem-pants. Obligingly, our neighbours were discussing their congress.

'Violet made a fine job of it,' said one of them.

'Well,' said another, 'I don't think she should have been in the chair ... certainly not at the inaugural meeting. She's only been an acolyte six weeks.'

'Quite right,' agreed a third member of the party. 'In my opinion some people have been getting their promotion too fast. Look at Irma becoming a priestess.'

'That's the fault of that creature Ashraf.'

'She's a honey,' said an obviously deaf old lady.

'Ashraf! Why, I don't know what possessed the Grand Master to appoint *her* Executive Priestess.'

'She does the Mysteries real nice.'

'*I* would do the Mysteries well for twenty thousand bucks a year ... *and* expenses.'

'Gee, not so loud! Ashraf's sitting right behind you.'

All three of us turned. Ashraf, the Executive Priestess, looked magnificent – and extremely attractive – in a jewelled, flame-coloured sari.

'It's May!' exclaimed Vera. 'May Tinker!'

Before I could reach the Executive Priestess's table she had fled through a door at the back of the restaurant which led into an alley full of Coca-Cola crates and trash cans. In the light of a street-lamp I could see movement among the overflow of litter, and there – emerging cautiously – I found Mattie. May's little hamster stepped on to my hand quite willingly. When I put him on our table he sat up on his hindlegs and washed behind the ears.

'I guess May didn't see us,' said Rand.

'I think she did,' contradicted Vera. 'Why did she chicken out, Mattie?'

Mattie, satisfied that his coat was immaculate, had nibbled the nearest table napkin and was beginning to make a nest for himself.

'Let's see if we can find May.' I put the hamster in my coat-pocket complete with damaged napkin. With luck we'd find May before Mattie discovered that threads from my suit would make a more luxurious nest.

Vera thought we should find out at which hotels the *Sisters of the Tibetan Truth* were staying, but I convinced her that May wouldn't have gone to her hotel if she really was dodging us. Rand suggested we should comb Virginia Street.

It was a tall order. Virginia Street consisted of vast gambling clubs, hall after hall open to the street, full of one-armed bandits, packed with the *Sisters of the Tibetan Truth*.

The only possibility of spotting any one person was to go right through the clubs. And the only way of looking like a respectable person going about his lawful business was to put coins in the machines; the sharp-eyed stewardesses and money-changers seemed suspicious of anyone who stood about without pumping a handle. So we pumped, and after a while Vera complained that her right arm was getting sore. We switched to left-handed machines, but even that became hard on the muscles.

'Let's go back to our hotel,' said Vera. 'May's probably right there, playing roulette.'

Just then Rand had won five dollars, and he seemed set on putting them back into the fruit-machines – at ten cents a pull. 'Go ahead,' he said, his eyes fixed on the somersaulting plums. 'I'll catch you up.'

'Look out for May.'

'Sure,' he promised, absent-mindedly.

May was not at the roulette-tables of the Golden Hotel, but Vera had 'a feeling' she might turn up for a game of blackjack. And since I'd never played blackjack she thought I should try my hand.

We wandered from table to table watching those pretty columns of silver dollars change places and owners. The *Sisters of the Tibetan Truth*, their peacock garments drooping, had begun to look solemn and mesmerized by the coins and the numbers and the speed with which the croupiers pushed the money around.

I made up my mind to lose five dollars and no more, and promptly made fifty. Pocketing a fast buck seemed wrong somehow, so I ordered some champagne and accepted the hospitality of Vera's room. That didn't seem exactly right either, especially when Vera changed into 'something comfortable', voluminous and transparent.

After the first bottle of champagne I was so hot that I had to take my coat off. So as not to disturb Mattie I carefully draped it over a chair. Mattie apparently didn't feel the loss of my warmth; he stayed asleep.

Vera, nicely arranged on her bed, told me to relax – which I did. Ensconced in my arms she kept sipping champagne, keeping her plunging neckline from plunging too low and keeping her hair from getting ruffled. American men, she told me, were horribly puritanical.

'What would you call ... what we're doing now, in England?'

I was none too sure. 'Making love?'

'There! You see the difference? Making love sounds real nice. *American* men would call it *having sex*. Isn't it disgusting?'

'Well ... we're *not* having sex, are we?'

'Ooh,' she shuddered. 'Don't mention that phrase to me ... I've met only two kinds of guys; Rand's type, who's scared stiff of women ... you *heard* what he said ... and the other kind who's just as scared but gets them – by filling up himself and the girl with vodka.'

'Vodka?' I watched her toss down the champagne.

'Sure. That's what everyone drinks nowadays.'

'So Russia's avenging herself on America.'

She giggled, and skilfully removed my hand from her leg. '*You* are different, Michael.'

'Don't be too sure. I'm not made of stone.'

'I know you aren't.' She sighed, shifted her weight from the right side of my chest to the left, and went to sleep.

In the morning Vera and Mattie had gone.

The writing on the dressing-table mirror, in lipstick, looked so familiar that my stomach turned over. And then, with real relief, I recognized Vera's room; so the writing *wasn't* Julia's. The message on the mirror was innocuous – just an invitation to breakfast in the coffee-bar.

On my way down I met the Mexican mother, returning from mass with a black lace-mantilla on her head, flanked by Micky Finn in an enormous new stetson and Huckleberry Hound wearing Indian moccasins of the kind Reno sold as souvenirs. Micky Finn's boots creaked as loudly as ever. The three of them had passed me, without a sign of recognition, when I realized that Micky Finn had held Mattie in his hands.

I caught them up outside their room. 'Hi, Micky!'

'Yeah?'

'Micky, this hamster here belongs to me. May I have him back?'

'No.'

'I'll give you something for finding him.'

'What?'

I took out half a dollar.

'No.' He clutched Mattie more tightly.

'All right ... a silver dollar.'

Micky Finn looked at his mother.

'*Madre de Diós,*' she scolded, 'take it. Ask them to change it and go to the children's room ... you may play the machines until I fetch you.'

'Fruit-machines?' I asked, still with the dollar in my hand.

'Sure.' The mother snatched the coin and the hamster in one movement.

'But, señora! Is that wise? As you said, your husband gambles...'

'On *horses*,' she snapped, pushing Mattie at me. 'Micky! Go play!'

Neither Vera nor Rand were in the coffee-bar, but in a corner half hidden by plastic tulips I saw May – in a severe grey suit.

'Gee, thanks,' she said, when I delivered her hamster. This time she made no attempt to run away.

'Why did you disappear last night?' I asked her.

'Well ... I was dressed.'

'You're ... wearing something now, aren't you?'

'You don't understand, Michael ... I was kinda on the job.'

'As Executive Priestess.'

'How d'you know?'

'Some of the *Sisters of the Tibetan Truth* were talking of you.'

'*They* would ... though they're all real nice,' she added, generously.

'What kind of society is it?'

'It's a new doctrine called *self-knowledge*. You think about yourself to get yourself straightened out. It's great, the way you can adjust once you *know* you're jealous, or greedy. Get it?'

'I think so. What are the Mysteries you perform?'

'Oh, the girls shouldn't gas about that.' She looked genuinely shocked. 'Nor about the Grand Master who's formulated our doctrine.'

'May one know who he is?'

'Why, yes. Abdul Karim Kochbar ... from Tibet.'

The name sounded familiar. 'Has he ... formulated a doctrine on training animals too?'

'Sure. He's written a book about how to treat them. You see it's all kinda tied in with self-knowledge and the Tibetan Truth doctrine,' May explained excitedly. 'Take Mattie here ... Abdul gave him to me. And do you know why? Because he's the humblest creature of all ... just a little mouse.'

'The most delinquent, unhumble mouse I've ever met.'

May ignored that. 'And this humble mouse must be right here with me to remind me that though I'm the Executive Priestess I'm just nothin' ... I must forget I ever was a film star or I'll forget the Tibetan Truth and be back where I started.'

'Is it all right for an Executive Priestess to have a mink-covered antique telephone?' I inquired. 'It isn't exactly a humble thing to have in your office.'

May frowned. 'I guess it *must* be ... *Abdul* wanted me to have a telephone that's kinda different.'

'For receiving Tibetan Truths, I suppose.'

'I guess so. You *are* clever, Michael. I never thought of it that way. You see, Abdul's just great. He thinks of everything ... like giving me Mattie because the emblem of Tibetan Truth is the humble little mouse, and ...'

'Where *is* Mattie?'

'Over there ... by the coffee-machine.'

Before I had reached the counter, where Mattie appeared to be wrestling with a power-cable, there was a brilliant flash followed by an explosion overhead. I grabbed the hamster and gave him back to May. Everyone, staff and customers, was gazing at the ceiling; it seemed a good time for leaving.

In the foyer Vera and Rand were having their bags carried to the car. 'Michael, where have you been? We've been looking for you,' said Vera.

'I was in the coffee-bar. Your lipstick message ...'

The tip of Vera's shoe jabbed at my ankle. 'We're ready to go. Are you?'

As I carried down my bags, the lifts being apparently out of order, the roaring I'd heard in the coffee-bar became louder. Two or three Ophelias, screaming vigorously, went flying past me into the lobby. Porters and waiters, money-changers and croupiers were dashing about in a panic.

'What is it?' asked Vera.

'What is it?' asked May, coming out of the coffee-bar, hamster in hand.

'It's Mattie, I expect,' I told her.

'What's he done?'

'I don't know ... but you'd better take him away, quietly.'

63

'Fire!' yelled a man in a tuxedo.

'Fire?' asked an aged Ophelia. 'Did you say fire?'

There was more rushing and squealing; only the people feeding the one-armed bandits carried on putting in their nickels and quarters – distant-eyed, completely absorbed.

'Let's get outa here,' said Rand.

We hadn't driven more than two blocks when the Golden Hotel burst into flames.

CHAPTER SIX

We saw a variety of monuments to destruction and decay on the road between Reno and the Nevada desert, a trail of sad dumps occasionally enlivened by cats' cradles of coloured pennants. There were car-dumps of coupés crumpled and concertinaed like wastepaper, dumps of flattened cars, dumps where cars stood around rotting away – their bonnets open like the beaks of hungry fledglings – and dumps where the cars had just fallen to bits like stately homes that had been taxed out of existence. There were sinister dumps of bathtubs, modern cookers, modern refrigerators, English prams and army-equipment.

Destruction in the Nevada desert, Rand told us, was of the invisible kind; at least, we did not *see* atomic mushrooms or radio-active dust. But somewhere along those miles of sand and rock 'clean' atomic explosions were being carried out which – according to the defence experts – caused only negligible increases in the radio-activity of the area.

'Nothing to worry about,' said Rand, stepping on the accelerator, 'though all that atomic crap makes me feel like tumbleweed.'

The tumbleweed, great balls of it bowling along the road, looked comical and fantastic and pathetically solitary. Occasionally a balloon of that straw-like weed would lose its way in the scrub or get spiked on the wires of a fence. With luck it would take root until another wind sent it dancing through the desert but more often it just withered in captivity. I could see why the atomic crap made Rand feel like tumbleweed.

The change-over from the desert to the high mountains of the Sierra Nevada was fast and fabulous – truly American. Within a couple of hours we had to put on sun-glasses to protect ourselves from a hot, dust-laden wind *and* keep them on against the glare of snow. The Sierra with its

65

sportsman-dotted ski slopes, ski-lifts, frozen lakes and week-end chalets looked like a chunk of Switzerland which had emigrated to better itself.

In Sacramento, the state capital of California, the streets were lined with palm-trees and we were in high summer. And in San Francisco we drove into the nearest thing to a chilly, foggy, London spring evening.

San Francisco was a place for eating, said Vera. So we went for *smorgasbrød* to the Jack Tar, a vast sky-scraper of which the San Franciscans disapprove because it is built in the Los Angeles style. After Vera had helped herself from the buffets several times we went to the Chinese quarter, drank tea and wandered around admiring temples and minute children in Chinese dress. Around midnight Vera was hungry again, so we drove to the Fishermen's Wharf and ordered a *bouillabaisse*. By then Vera was in a black mood again. Gazing at the floodlit fishing-boats she attacked Rand for his calamitous table-manners; why couldn't he use his knife instead of *butchering* his squid? When he pointed out, quite reasonably, that she wasn't using her knife either, she demanded to be taken back to our hotel.

In the morning she said she couldn't possibly arrive in Santa Monica with her hair looking like an abandoned bird's-nest and asked to be driven to a place which turned out to be the *Chinese Facial Beatifying Company*. The hair-stylist, a Mr McKlotsky, told us she would be finished in two hours, and she asked us to meet her on top of the Fairmount Hotel.

Rand and I parked the car on the tenth floor of a garage and strolled through the shopping centre. I wanted stockings of a new shade for Julia. Rand interpreted between me and the saleswoman; what I wanted was *hose*. He asked me what size Vera took, did not believe me when I said the hose was for my fiancée in England, and bought a couple of identical pairs. Next I bought a pearl on a gold-chain. Rand bought the same.

A notice opposite the jewel-shop made me stop in the middle of the sidewalk. It said *No Down On Vets*. That seemed pretty decent to me – someone actually advertising his good feelings towards my profession. But Rand put me right: Vets in America weren't veterinary surgeons but war-veterans, and the notice meant there was a hospital where veterans did not have to pay a deposit. Apparently sick people usually had to pay *before* being admitted to hospital.

Perhaps the patients could afford it. At least the women we saw looked prosperous enough; many of them, carrying shopping-bags, were wearing mink-stoles and flowered hats – expensively fragile frivolities. Julia would have called such morning opulence dowdy. Another thing that surprised me were the seals – like seals – padding about the beach or leaping from the rocks; it seemed very brave of them to play so close to the fur-minded girls.

All those fragments of a strange city fell into place when we met Vera in the cocktail-lounge of the Fairmount. The lift which took us up through a wonderfully tall glass-tube on the outside of the skyscraper revealed a place of grandeur and beauty, the city with its steep streets, the water-ways – like the Norwegian fjords in sunlight, the charming curves and contours of wooded hills. Because it was so admirable we stayed too long on the rotating observation-bar and drank too many cocktails, and when we got down among the traffic again I kept thinking of Walt Disney's lion, acknowledged master of man and beast, who got scared stiff of the cars that bared their teeth at him in Fifth Avenue.

The number-plate of Rand's car was FAT606, and as we drove towards Los Angeles he told us he would not register another car in the State of California until the system was changed; he found three-letter words objectionable.

Vera laughed. 'You *don't* belong to that number-plate vigilance society, do you?'

'No, not yet.'

'Rand! If you join I'll never drink another cocktail with you.'

'Well, if the three-letter words don't bother you they sure embarrass a lot of other people.'

'What's wrong with FAT?'

'It's kinda physical, isn't it? How do you think a fat guy

would feel driving this car?'

'Oh!' Vera groaned. 'Why must *some* people be so self-conscious? So people have bodies, and they're physical, but why be puritanical about words that remind them of what they are?'

'Go ahead, read the number-plates.'

We all did. The letters read SEX, BRA, DAM, SAP, SOT, BED.

'I suppose,' said Vera, 'BED is objectionable.'

'It shouldn't be on a car.'

'Nuts ... WED, ALE ... BAG ... BEG ... CAD,' Vera read out. 'Nothing nasty about those, is there?'

'RUM ... DUD,' Rand continued the list of passing cars, 'HAG ... RAW ... GOD ... If it isn't vulgar it's sacrilege or something.'

'Or something,' mimicked Vera. 'Why don't you grow up!'

'Have you thought about foreigners?' asked Rand, mildly.

'What foreigners?'

'The ones that come to California ... like Michael. Maybe – say RAW or BEG – means something real bad in another language.'

'Michael speaks English.'

'Other foreigners don't.'

'Two- or four-letter words might mean something even worse if you start in on foreign languages.'

'Four-letter words *would* be worse,' agreed Rand. 'But there must be some system that cuts out what is ... improper.'

'Is SAG improper?' asked Vera.

'Sure.'

'So that's the way your mind works! Know something? *Sag* makes me think of shopping ... carrying a net full of parcels.'

Rand, sliding deeper into the driving-seat, fell silent. The cars had put on their lights; instead of fast-moving three-letters words we saw large luminous snakes in red and white parallel lines speeding between the high hills and a cityful of neon signs.

WESTERN EXTERMINATORS struck me as a strange welcome to Hollywood, but a mile or so nearer Los Angeles more signs flickered and darted about the sky: NUTSHOP ... BODYSHOP ... RESTAURANT, THE BROKEN DRUM. YOU CAN'T BEAT IT ... UNDERTAKER UTTER MCKINLEY UNDERSTANDS.

'Rand,' said Vera, in a small voice, 'don't let's stop anywhere down-town. It would give Michael a wrong impression.'

We passed streets full of pawnshops and street-corners crowded with teenagers. Boys and girls wore what looked like a uniform of jeans and T-shirts with a name printed across the chest; names democratically included Mozart, James Dean, Einstein and Raquel Welsh.

Within half an hour we were back in a stream of traffic, moving swiftly through the parts of Los Angeles which looked more like feudal estates than suburbs, travelling through whiffs of scent from flowering gardens, from parks and the Pacific Ocean. I was beginning to understand why sixteen hundred people a day were migrating from the rest of America to California.

The legendary Sunset Boulevard with its beautiful and ugly houses, magnificent and hideous apartment-blocks, its villages, beaches, factories, car-dumps and orchards seemed to go on for dozens of miles. The drive became even more bewildering when Rand took a right turn bouncing the car up a steep, narrow road to an isolated hill.

The tall iron gates at the top opened automatically; our headlights picked out a fox strolling across the drive, a night-bird in flight, the façade of a white mansion. With the engine switched off the silence was deafening. Against the continuous high-pitched hum of the cicadas we heard the 'coo-hoo, coo-hoo' of a burrowing owl and the talented solo of a mocking-bird imitating the voices of titmice and nuthatches, orioles and fox-sparrows – 'te-te weet-wet', 'kip', 'sick-a-thee-thee-thee', 'sicka-a-thee-thee-thee'.

'Albert!' shouted a powerful female voice, 'Albert! Put on yer socks! They're here!'

A searchlight blinded me, and when I opened my eyes again the house and the gardens stood out illuminated by dozens of concealed blue reflector-lamps. Everything looked as if it were made of crystal glass. But there was nothing ethereal about the dogs which hurtled out to welcome us.

'I'm partial to animals, sir,' said Masters, 'but Madam's little terriers are not – to put it frankly – ideal travelling companions. Especially Manila, sir ... she was sick. And if you don't mind my mentioning it, I don't believe she's quite herself yet.'

'She's going to have pups,' I told him.

'Madam didn't inform me.' Masters sounded aggrieved. 'And Madam's given me a message for you, sir. She hopes you and Mr Rand will be able to commence with the preliminary organization of the *Wee Souls' Sanctuary*. The accommodation will be in English style; there won't be any need for new kennels. When you survey the grounds you will find sundry buildings perfectly suitable for animals ... Whisky and water, sir?'

'Thank you, Masters.'

'No ice ... naturally?'

'No ice.'

'*Albert's* attending to the ... cocktails for Mr Rand and Miss Vera.'

The two of them had gone to clean up, leaving me in a fifty-foot lounge of such character that I promised myself photographs of it. The semi-circular bay overlooking the lights of Santa Monica and, presumably, the ocean, had enormous floor-to-ceiling windows alternating with walls showing the natural stone. White leather-covered benches, curved, and eight to twelve feet long, lined the walls and the horseshoe-shaped tables were made of rose-quartz or white marble. In the centre of the room, surrounded by a deep white carpet, stood a marble-fountain with a metal-lined bowl. Judging by the canopy it could be converted to an open fire. It was the clever use of textures and proportions that gave the room its style; the only colours in it were a few touches of green and blue in cushions, lamps and paintings by Rothko, Kandinsky and Modigliani.

Thinking of the Duke's fifteenth-century cottage, which a workman had described as one of the dirtiest old holes in England, with tons of dust inside the walls, I wondered what the Duke would make of his wife's summer residence. He was bound to be misled by the fact that it was called *The Cottage*, while his own little shack went by the grand name of *Northwing, Hazelbridge House*. But perhaps the year the Duke had spent as a guest of various embassies had accustomed him to luxury and space. Certainly his man, Masters, seemed at home at *The Cottage*.

Albert came in, followed by a sun-burnt little maid carrying a tray of glasses. Her fingernails were at least an inch long.

'That's Jackie,' he introduced her.

'Hi,' said Jackie.

Albert took the tray from her and set it down in front of me. 'You can go, Jackie ... She just knocks me out,' he shook his head, and grinned. 'My Lovely – that's my wife Greta, I always call her my Lovely – well, she says the girl's dumb. I don't think she is. I guess she's a real good business-woman; don't do any work, keeps her nails smooth, then she goes and sells them for ten dollars a set.'

'She *sells* her fingernails?'

'Sure, Mr Morton. They're made into false nails ... I reckon there's a demand for them right close to us, over in Hollywood ... My Lovely figures you wouldn't mind a cold supper ... She's a Londoner ...'

The Lovely herself came stomping in. She was a head taller than her husband, about twice his weight, and she had large hands and feet even for a woman her size. 'Don't 'old with cold stuff,' she informed me, 'but Albert 'ere forgot ter get the meat. So it's 'am, sir. No memory ... that's the trouble with Albert. But I've made ye a nice suet-pudding ... nothing like suet-pudding when you're feeling home-sick. Any time I start moping my Albert always says, "Go on, Lovely, make yourself a suet-pud" ... Jackie!' her voice rose as high as the mocking-bird's outside. 'You'll be in trouble, my girl! Told 'er to lay the table, I did. But it's dreaming, dreaming all day with them American girls ... 'ollywood, that's what's *their* trouble ... Albert, don't stand there like a statue. Put the wine in the bucket.'

Rand tore apart a soft roll. 'Where's Vera?'

'Gone shopping.' We were having breakfast in a kitchen that was fitted out like a milk-bar. The expresso-machine gurgled, the grill – encased in glass – made little exploding sounds, the dish-washing machine chugged, the oven sighed and an amplifier moaned out the ubiquitous 'sweet' music. Outside the crickets had taken over from the cicadas, a golden-crowned sparrow was singing 'Three Blind Mice' and the sun, at summer-strength, was silent. At least I thought I couldn't hear it make a noise.

'Was she annoyed?' asked Rand.

'Vera? No. Why? What have you done to her?'

Rand looked at me, dolefully. 'I guess she wouldn't notice if I did try doing something.'

'Have you given her the presents you bought in San Francisco?'

'Yeah.'

'What did she say?'

'Nothin' much ... They're still lying on the hall-table upstairs, where she put them down.'

'If you've finished let's go and look at the kennels.' I thought it was time Rand had something to do.

'Sure.'

There was plenty of room for keeping dogs well exercised – lawns, copses and a steep but not dangerous hillside. 'What do you think of the Duchess's name for her kennels?' I asked.

'Okay.'

'The *Wee Souls' Sanctuary Inc.* sounds to me more suitable for a pets' cemetery.'

'That's what I thought. But the Duchess said this guy Abdul Karim Kochbar – the one with the doctrine for animals – suggested it. He feels it would make the animal-owners realize that this place recognizes how dogs have souls, and the Duchess will cater for their spirits while the dogs are in training.'

'We'd better meet this fellow.'

'How about that!' Rand had stopped at the sight of a building which looked like a miniature mosque complete with onion-domes and a muezzin. 'Maybe it *is* meant to be kennels.'

It obviously was. The other buildings we found were follies as well – replicas of a Tudor cottage, a Swiss chalet, a Chinese temple, gipsy-caravans and a Norman tower.

Even Rand looked amused. 'That's great, just great! So that's what the Duchess calls "accommodation in English style". Is *this* the kinda kennels you have in England?'

'No, not quite. She should call it an ex-Empire style.'

'What will the dogs think of it?'

'They won't mind.'

'I guess they'll adjust,' Rand agreed, 'that is, if that guy Abdul's training-methods aren't too screwy. We could drive over and talk to him.'

We strolled back towards the house, past the mosque and the Norman tower, past lilacs, standard roses, jacaranda trees, scarlet and orange bird-of-paradise blooms, gladioli and daffodils all flowering indiscriminately, side by side, as if there were no such thing as seasons.

Rand was about to drive his car out of the garage when a big alsatian came bounding up the drive. It was wearing a pair of red pants with the initials D.A.F. and it was obviously not liking the garment. Halting a few feet away from us it kept twisting about, contorting its neck to bite the pants, snapping at its back and hind-legs.

'Come here, boy!' I called.

The dog had stopped its antics and snarled.

'Come on. Let's take this thing off.'

Rand looked at the angry animal, and at me. And then, fatalism defeating caution, he climbed out of the car. 'Okay. You take off his pants. I'll hold him.'

'*I'd* better hold him.'

'I've already *got* a lot of scars.'

'He won't bite me.'

Rand edged towards the dog's back. 'Well, watch yourself.'

I pounced at the muzzle and at the same time wedged the dog's shoulders between my knees. He couldn't bite, but the powerful body struggled and twisted so frenziedly that it became a battle between us. It was by no means certain which would win. Rand was almost knocked down twice before he succeeded in peeling off those stretch-nylon pants.

I kept talking to the alsatian and gradually he calmed down sufficiently to look me in the face. As he became aware of his freed hindquarters the muscles relaxed, I could lessen my hold on his body and eventually release the dog altogether. I expected him to bolt; instead he took a sniff at Rand and myself, wagged his tail and allowed himself to be stroked. He looked quite disappointed when we drove away.

'Wonder where *he* came from,' said Rand.

It did not take us long to find out. Half a mile down the hill we came upon a signpost pointing to a lane which ran almost parallel to the road leading to *The Cottage. Decent Animals Federation* it said in newly-painted letters.

Rand put his foot on the brake. 'Isn't this the organization Gay Petrell's crazy about?'

I thought it was. 'There can't be two like it. Let's take a look.'

'Kinda awkward.'

'We can give them the pants we took off the alsatian.'

A short distance from the signpost the lane curved away from the grounds of *The Cottage* but there was no doubt that the *Decent Animals Federation*'s land adjoined the Duchess's estate and the imminent *Wee Souls' Sanctuary Inc.* We drove past a couple of new kennel-buildings, along a weedy drive to a dilapidated frame-house. Rotten boards were hanging from its sides, the balcony above the porch had tilted forward at a perilous angle, but someone had hung from it an expensive neon sign, *Buck House, D.A.F.* The feudal-looking crest beneath consisted of a couple of dogs rampant in full military cloaks apparently supporting an extremely straight, muscle-bound knight with a raised sword.

'Dressed-up dogs and the *naked* sword,' observed Rand.

Since no one answered the door he reversed the car. I had just got in beside him when an enormous laurel-bush beside the house parted, revealing a gaunt, rather hatchet-faced man in full Highland dress, tormenting the set of bagpipes under his arm. He got to the point of extracting a squeak and then, for some reason, desisted from playing the thing.

'And what would ye be wantin'?' He bawled at us in a Clyde-side accent. 'This is prrivate properrty.'

I took the alsatian's pants from my pocket. 'We want to return a piece of your property. I suppose this *is* yours.'

'Aye.' He snatched the pants out of my hand. 'And what have ye done with Plato?'

'If Plato's your dog he'll be somewhere on this hill,' I told him, 'calming down. The pants you put on him were driving him out of his mind.'

'*Trews*,' corrected the Lowlander. 'They're trews. Aye. and ye had nae right te strip the paer brute naked.'

'Poor brute's right,' said Rand. 'I figure if you keep putting clothes on him he'll go berserk and attack somebody, some day.'

'Ye've no' been asked your opinion, laddie.' The Lowlander made the 'laddie' sound quite offensive. 'Our President won't allow naked animals here ... aye, even though we're on our own properrty here ... If ye ever find an animal of ours again don't ye lay hands on its trews. Returrn it to *me*.'

The man's arrogance had become too much for me. 'You'd better keep your animals in your own grounds,' I told him, 'if you can get them to stay.'

Not an auspicious neighbourhood for the Duchess's dog-training school, I thought, as we left *Buck House*. The Lowlander could be heard tormenting his bagpipes and from one of the kennels came the long sad howls of a dog.

Many of the drivers in the long line of traffic that trundled along the coast between Santa Monica and Venice appeared to be naked. The sunburnt torsos and shoulders gave a pleasingly casual land-of-the-free air to the hot day.

'They *are* wearing bathers,' Rand assured me. 'And shoes.'

'Why shoes?'

'Gotta wear shoes. There's a by-law. If a cop catches you driving in bare feet you get fined.'

I said that didn't make sense; with bare feet one had the perfect grip on brakes and clutch.

'Sure,' agreed Rand. 'But how about *that*? In Connecticut

75

a man who kisses his wife in public, on a Sunday, can be jailed for indecent behaviour.'

'Absurd.'

'*I* got arrested for indecent exposure first time I was in New York. Know why? There was a heat-wave ... I walked in Central Park with the first three buttons of my shirt undone. I guess I was about sixteen then ... It *doesn't* make sense, but maybe it'll make you understand about organizations like the *Decent Animals Federation*. Societies like that aren't just crazy. They're sad ... real sad.'

In Venice there was a selection of very different but equally touching societies ... The Church of Job, The Temple of Absalom, The Brotherhood of Hamath, The Gospellers of Matthew, dozens of sectarian houses wedged in among synagogues, Catholic, Anglican, Presbyterian and other widely-accepted churches. There, on the beach facing the Pacific Ocean, this catering for the need to have a faith rather than a good meal struck me as desperate *and* sad.

Rand's car turned inland and to the right into a road running parallel to the ocean. Suddenly we were in the middle of a caricature of Venice, Italy. Someone had actually built a wrought-iron and stucco Piazza San Marco and furnished the covered walks with coffee-bars, hardware-shops, hamburger counters and Coca-Cola stands. The roads leading off the Piazza were even weirder, consisting of little frame or brick houses with backyards. And the back-yards seemed to be populated with black giant grasshoppers. Seen against the sky the things kept pumping up and down in perpetual motion, looking like robot-invaders from another planet.

Rand was enjoying my surprise. 'Crazy, isn't it?'

'What are they?'

'Obscene grasshoppers ... pumping oil out of the ground. How would *you* like to have an oil well in your backyard? ... I didn't. These things going up and down, day and night, get kinda scarey. So I moved into a big apartment-block where I see nothing but people and pets.'

Abdul Karim Kochbar, author of the *Doctrinum Animalis Psychologicum*, seemed to have found himself the one establishment away from the oilpumps and the religious organizations. Driving through an archway formed by the gilt-letters SELFKNOWLEDGE we found ourselves in a little park of palm-trees and flowering shrubs. A small villa, reminiscent of an Eastern temple, cast its white reflection into a water-lily pond; an exotic chant came floating across a hedge of flowering bougainvillea. Behind the hedge we came upon a building which was the nearest thing I'd seen in the States to an English surburban brick bungalow.

Before I could touch the bell the door swung open. Something black and hairy brushed my face and Rand let out a yell of alarm.

'I say, I'm frightfully sorry,' said an urbane, English voice.

My eyes were getting accustomed to the darkness of the house. Mr Abdul Karim Kochbar, unmistakably an Indian, was wearing a Rugby tie. He sounded like a man entitled to wear it.

'This animal of mine's a bit rough on strangers.' He tugged at the black pelt of the creature whose arms were still encircling Rand's neck. It turned out to be a medium-sized orang-utan. 'I hope Saint Cheetah hasn't bruised you. She doesn't mean to hurt people. She's just getting rather big.'

'Okay,' gasped Rand.

'Won't you come in?'

The Indian led us into an office full of filing-cabinets, stacked newspapers and books. 'Take a pew.' He made room on a black sofa. 'I'll stop the row.' The chant, emanating from a record-player, ceased. 'Of course, I know who you are ... The Duchess of Alanspring's written to me about her project. Good idea, don't you think?'

'That depends on what your training-methods are,' I said.

'I don't suppose you've read my book.'

'We ... looked through it.'

Abdul nodded. 'Well, actually no one reads it. At least I haven't met anyone who's read it.'

'We got the hang of it,' I assured him. 'But we thought we might discuss a few details.'

'Certainly ... You've just come from England?'

'A fortnight ago.'

'Tell me, how's Lord Cabbott? Has he got over his slipped disc?'

I told him I didn't know Lord Cabbott.

He looked slightly disappointed. 'The Establishment still going strong?'

'It was a month ago.'

'Frightfully good show, don't you think? I used to go there with Tony.'

The gentle inquisition to discover whether or not I was 'top-drawer' continued. I was too amused to get annoyed. Abdul was no more foolish than many English people I knew who were abysmally ignorant about the social attitudes of Scotsmen like myself. How was I to convey to such people that I regarded the top-drawer as a somewhat absurd piece of furniture or that I'd never felt the need to establish my identity by surrounding it with other identities?

'... couldn't go to New York,' Abdul was saying, 'owing to pressure of work. I hear Tiger's play was quite brilliant. You didn't see it by any chance?'

'I did.'

'You *know* Claire and Tiger?'

'Yes, yes I know them.'

At last Abdul had become aware that the inquisition had gone far enough. 'I rather miss England, you know.'

'Then why not live there?'

'My work's *here*.'

'The *Doctrinum Animalis Psychologicum*?'

Abdul smiled. 'Ghastly title; and quite inaccurate. Latin wasn't my best subject at school. As a matter of fact I did want to change the title, but I left it too late; the book came out sooner than I'd expected ... Actually the animal-training thing is only a small part of my work. I'm chiefly concerned with people ... American women to be precise.'

'The *Sisters of the Tibetan Truth*?'

'Exactly ... the *Self-knowledge Doctrine*.'

'Very interesting.'

'Not for you of course.' Abdul grabbed his orang-utan, which had again taken to hugging Rand. 'Saint Cheetah ... keep still, you monkey ... As I was saying, self-knowledge

78

... the idea of understanding one's self wouldn't be new to someone like you.'

'Is it new to American women?'

'The whole of America needs self-knowledge, but since this is a matriarchal society one has to begin with the women ... Don't you think people here should be able to understand why they treat *imperialism* as a dirty word when they themselves are frantically busy pinching other peoples' empires for themselves?'

'Are they?' asked Rand.

'Of course. Take my own country ... Do you know what Henry Miller said as far back as 1934 ... Henry Miller, the *American* writer? He said, "India's enemy is not England, but America. India's enemy is the time-spirit, the hand which cannot be turned back. Nothing will avail to offset this virus which is poisoning the whole world. America is the very incarnation of doom. She will drag the whole world down to the bottomless pit." ... You'll find it on page eighty-six of *Tropic of Cancer*. So much for imperialism.' Abdul removed Saint Cheetah from his record-player. 'Then there are the American self-delusions such as human rights ... rather sad when you consider the position of the American Negro. Equally awful is the American puritanism. Deep down the majority of people revolt against hundreds of silly taboos; they're justly angry. But their anger is suppressed – the system of conformity makes certain of that – so the anger becomes a deep-seated longing for violence ... sheer brute violence. The people here are thrilled by reports of murder and revolutions ... such tales release some of the pressures inside them. Well, *my* view is that the frustrations should be relieved by more normal methods; *self-knowledge* is the most logical beginning.'

It seemed logical enough until I remembered the houris and Ophelias at Reno. 'If you have a serious purpose,' I said, 'why do you put your poor old women into fancy-dress?'

'The symbol is one of the oldest methods for engaging people's emotions and beliefs.'

'Is the mink-covered antique telephone a symbol too?'

'Certainly ... As a matter of fact May told me you helped her choose her instrument.'

'I suppose your Executive Priestess is another symbol.'

Abdul stroked his restless monkey. 'She's a dear girl, don't you think? Rather a bore that I can't marry her ... The trouble is there's nothing mystic about a *husband*. And she's got to keep her sense of the mystic ... it comes over with great conviction when she does the rites. *The Sisters of the Tibetan Truth* couldn't do without this element in the doctrine, at the moment. The last Executive Priestess I engaged made a terrible hash of the Mysteries.'

Rand got up. The unflagging attentions of Saint Cheetah had become too much for him. 'Sure, sure. You've got a point. Maybe there are *some* doctrines we can use in the States. But what's it got to do with the Duchess's dog-training place?'

'Her Grace appears to agree with me that one must know how to bring up animals ... it's a beginning to a better understanding of one's self ... I won't explain my theory now ... No doubt there'll be other opportunities. The Duchess has appointed me her consultant to the new establishment. Of course, I won't interfere with your arrangements until the animals are actually in residence as it were.'

As we shook hands with Abdul, Saint Cheetah tried to make off with Rand's handkerchief. The Indian, with admirable agility, retrieved it. 'I say, Saint Cheetah really is a bit of a monkey. Maybe I should try out my training-doctrine on her before I tackle the Duchess's dogs.'

Back at *The Cottage* the alsatian Plato, still trouserless, was hiding under Vera's garden-swing while Sam Bagshot junior was catechizing Vera.

'Ma'am, do you realize how many auto-accidents are caused by drivers being distracted by unclothed animals?'

'No.' Vera threw herself back, setting the swing in motion without in any way disturbing Plato. 'But if you put pants on animals doesn't it interefere with their natural functions?'

Sam Bagshot, who had been gazing at Vera's bare legs, blushed. 'No ... But that's beside the point...' He became aware of Rand and me. 'Why, you're the veterinarian from England, aren't you?' Looking at Vera like a man about to score a point, he added, 'I remember his attending a meeting of mine in New York. He promised to set up a branch of the *Decent Animals Federation* in London.'

'Did you, Michael?' asked Vera.

'No. Mr Bagshot suggested it.'

'I thought it was settled ... No matter.' The burly President of the D.A.F. quickly recovered his assurance. 'For the moment we're concerned with the Santa Monica branch of D.A.F. ... As I was suggesting to this young lady, we just can't have an establishment right next door to our kennels which allows its animals to go about naked ... I mean unclothed.'

'Well, you've got it,' said Vera.

Sam Bagshot ignored her remark. 'I guess it wouldn't be reasonable of us to expect you to go to the expense of buying clothes for your dogs. So, for the sake of good neighbourliness, I'm willing to supply you with appropriate garments. Naturally, in return, my Federation would expect you to put up one of our neon-signs showing that you are affiliated to us.'

'We're not,' said Vera.

'We can soon put that right.' Sam Bagshot produced a printed form from his pocket and a ball-point pen. 'Just sign here.'

'No thanks.' Vera made the swing fly up, displaying a lot of nicely shaped leg. 'Our dogs wouldn't like pants any more than your alsatian.'

'By now Plato would have been real comfortable in his trews if someone hadn't forcibly removed them.' Sam Bagshot took a pair of red pants from his pocket and showed them to the dog. 'Here, Plato!'

Plato flattened himself to the lawn.

'Come here boy!'

The dog gave a low growl. Sam, not devoid of courage, grabbed the animal's hind-quarters. The growling became fierce.

Vera took a backward swing, sending the President sprawling. 'You leave that dog alone! This isn't a sanitarium for people who get themselves bitten.'

Sam Bagshot picked himself up. 'You have no right, no

right at all, to coerce our animals.'

'No one's invited your dog,' said Vera, 'and no one's trying to keep him here. Just take him away.'

Sam gripped the plaited-leather lead he'd been holding in his hand and started to belabour as much of the dog as he could reach. The dog began to bark, and Vera to move the swing. The President had to get out of the way. 'You're being unco-operative,' he complained.

'Take it easy.' Vera herself looked none too easy. 'You can maltreat dogs at your own place if you're that kind of a guy. But you're not doing it here. Now, beat it.'

'This is ... I've never...' Sam Bagshot spluttered, 'I ... I'm going to see my attorney.'

'You do that,' said Vera, stroking Plato's head.

We watched the President's car roar down the drive.

Rand shook his head. 'You were kinda rough on him, Vera.'

'Oh, you!' she turned on him, 'You aren't much help, are you?'

CHAPTER SEVEN

'Why are you being so unkind to Rand?' I asked Vera.

'Rand?' She slid to a more comfortable position on my lap. Sunlight and the slats of the venetian blinds drew a pattern of tiger-stripes across her body. The big lounge was cool and quiet. 'He was okay when I was at college. I used to think he was kinda treasurely.'

'He is.'

'Nuts.' She rubbed her nose against my ear. 'He wants to have sex; *you* make love.'

I wished *someone* would come in; I was the last man to snub an attractive girl. The midday silence ticked on. Maybe Julia was right about me; perhaps it *was* my fault that I got cornered by young wildcats like Vera.

She gave a sigh and playfully rolled off my lap on to the white rug. The situation was becoming perilous, and the whole house appeared to be sleep-bound. The only sign of a presence apart from us was the distant voice of the Negro handyman Jeremiah swinging 'Oh Lord our help in ages past'.

'Rand's done jolly well,' I said, almost choking with my own heartiness. 'I wouldn't call Jeremiah and Albert *workers*, yet Rand managed to get them to put up wire-netting right round the estate ... all in a couple of days.'

'A lot of good *that* is.' Vera rolled over and put an arm round Plato, who was lying under the nearest marble table. '*He* is still with us.' It was true; since the fences had been put up we had relieved Plato of two pairs of pants. Not that we'd wanted to do it, but none of us had been capable of watching Plato's frenzied struggles with those ridiculous garments.

Vera took a letter from the pocket of her shorts. 'Here ... read.'

It was a letter from a firm of lawyers accusing Vera of deliberately withholding the alsatian Plato from his rightful owners, the *Decent Animals Federation*, of physically threatening the President of said Federation with a garden-swing and of using language inconsistent with good neigh-bourliness. The letter continued, 'However, our clients have generously decided not to proceed against you provided the coercion of the dog Plato on Tuesday, May 22, remains an isolated incident, and always provided your own animals do not offend the Members of D.A.F. by being seen in a state of indecent exposure.'

'Well?' Vera scratched Plato under the chin, a caress he particularly appreciated.

'Sam Bagshot's not *proceeding* against you because he hasn't got a case. But he soon will have, if you keep making a fuss of the dog.'

'Plato's cute ... we just can't kick him out.'

Jeremiah had stopped swinging his one and only tune. 'Oh Lord, our help in ages past,' came drifting over in a love-song croon.

'I know!' Vera sat up. 'We must train Plato to hide him-self when we tell him.'

'That's no solution.'

'Can you figure out anything better?'

'She's right.' Rand had come in from the garden. 'If we can't keep Plato outa here we must teach him how to make himself scarce.'

'Very well,' I agreed, 'but not here.'

'I guess not.' Rand glanced at the hill behind the house. 'That guy with the bagpipes might be out looking for Plato.'

'Let's go swimming,' suggested Vera.

'Great.' Rand's admiration was so obvious that Vera smiled. Holding out her hands to him she allowed him to pull her to her feet. Rand began to look quite lively. 'Sure, the beach is the place. Not many places where the dog can hide, so he'll have to be alert if he wants to get out of sight fast.'

As we piled flippers and beach-towels into the car it oc-curred to me that the Alanspring family had not brought me to America for the purpose of teaching a strange alsatian how to hide from its owners. But what could I do?

84

Plato didn't even have to be invited into Rand's car; he jumped in the back and settled down beside me as if he'd been used to accompanying us for years.

We had just driven out of the gates when Vera turned. 'Get lost!'

Luckily the tone of her voice conveyed the meaning. I picked up an armful of towels and threw myself on top of Plato. A second later the car passed our neighbour of the Highland dress.

There was no way of telling whether anyone among the sunbathers recognized Plato; we couldn't see their faces because they weren't wearing their own faces. We passed group after group of tanned bodies in swim-suits of every conceivable colour and style, all wearing different-coloured masks.

The sands were strewn with blue and red, yellow, green, purple and orange masks which, Vera told me, were made of plastic and had been designed by an artist who had spent five weeks sculpting them.

'If you put on a dark-coloured one,' explained Vera, 'you tan a light colour. If you cover up with a pale colour you turn dark.'

Tanning one's body seemed to be a strenuous ritual. There were men as well as girls with mirrors, metal-reflectors and even sheets of tin-foil contorting themselves to have the reflected sunrays play under their chins, in their armpits or along the side of their legs. They meant to look like evenly brown, perfectly fried sausages and apparently they didn't mind working at it.

The only people outside the masked crowds were teen-agers in identical blue jeans, all frayed at the ankles. They were the 'regulars' who had painted the names of their gangs on a part of the sea-wall which had become their own. The Titans sat beneath the letters TITANS and the Spartans beneath the legend SPARTANS; each group kept to itself, each occasionally sent off someone for Coca-Cola, each possessed a supply of comics, magazines or newspapers, at least one straw-hat and a transistor-radio.

We found a stretch of beach the sunbathers had shunned

because of the shingle and a specially large collection of empty beer-cans, and worked out our training-methods. I would show Plato a pair of the pants we had taken off him; Rand would give a warning-whistle – the first three notes of the *Stars and Stripes* – and then Vera would grab the dog and make him run away and hide. Before long, we hoped, Plato wouldn't need Vera's guidance and bolt by himself.

When Plato saw those pants in my hand his ears went up; he looked surprised but quite unworried. I moved closer, holding out the pants as if I intended putting them on. Plato put his head to one side and grinned, clearly regarding my manoeuvres as a joke between friends. Wasn't I the man who had relieved him more than once of those awful garments? There was nothing for it; I grabbed Plato, trying to get his hindquarters into the trews. The dog shook himself loose, and gave a delighted bark. This was a splendid game! He raced up to Rand, gambolled around Vera and jumped in the air trying to snatch the pants out of my hand.

At the end of a couple of hours we were hot and tired, Plato relaxed and contented. He still regarded us as friendly playmates but he had also begun to understand that we wanted him to behave in a certain manner. We had reached a point where Plato would quietly take note of the pants, prick up his ears at the whistle and allow Vera or Rand to lead him at the double behind the seawall or a beach-umbrella.

We went for a swim, intending to spend the rest of the afternoon on the beach. But it suddenly turned cold. A muddy-looking mist rolled across the water, shrouding everything from the coastline to the dedicated sun-worshippers. I rolled up in a towel, stripped off my wet bathing-trunks and put on trousers and shirt.

Suddenly I became aware of Rand staring at me. 'What's the matter?'

'Gee!' he breathed heavily. 'Don't do *that* again.'

'What?'

'You might have got arrested for indecency.'

'I didn't do anything indecent.'

'Really? You shouldn't change on the beach.'

'We might have gotten into real trouble,' said Vera. 'If anyone had noticed you changing ... There's Plato as well. We'd better not attract attention to *him*.'

Within three days Plato responded to the *Stars and Stripes*, whether Vera, Rand or I whistled the notes, and ran for cover with increasing speed and skill. There was only one other thing he had to be taught – to obey the signal no matter who whistled it. We decided to enlist the help of Albert and Lovely one day and Masters's assistance on another.

But the experiment had to be postponed. We were packing our beach-gear into the car, when a chauffeur-driven Cadillac drove up to *The Cottage*.

'Are you the Duchess of Alanspring, honey?' asked a stout lady with a head of grey curls.

'I'm her daughter,' said Vera.

'Glad to meet you.' The old lady produced a small white poodle with a hair-do as elaborate as her own. 'I'm Mrs Claude G. Blau junior. I guess you know I've come about your mother's advertisement. Do you know, honey, the moment I saw the name of your training-school I said to myself "Gracie, this is the place for your darling Gipsy." *Wee Souls' Sanctuary* is just a lovely name. I wouldn't dream of sending my Gipsy to a kennels ... but this is different; a little sanctuary looked after by a great lady who just adores animals.'

'Our charge is three hundred bucks ... dollars a month,' said Vera. 'That includes the training.'

'Oh, Gipsy's a perfect little lady,' said Mrs Claude G. Blau junior. 'There's only the littlest thing the matter with her ... she nibbles her nails. Can you cure that?'

'Sure,' said Rand. 'How long are you leaving Gipsy with us?'

'Three to four months. Mr Blau and I are going on a world tour ... I'd be real happy if I could see Gipsy's new little home.'

'We have a real nice surprise for you,' mimicked Vera, rather naughtily. Mrs Blau did not seem to notice. 'A genuine antique gipsy-caravan.'

'Now, isn't that just too thoughtful of you.'

We took client and poodle to the caravan-folly which, luckily, Jeremiah had fitted with wire-netting and wooden gates. Mrs Blau thought it cute. She thought her Gipsy would be happy at the *Wee Souls' Sanctuary Inc.* But before signing the kennel-contract she asked Vera whether she could meet the Duchess in person, before her departure. Knowing the Duchess would make her feel 'easy in her mind'.

By the time Mrs Claude G. Blau had departed and Gipsy was persuaded out of a fit of bad temper the afternoon had gone. We decided to put Plato through his paces on the lawn in front of the house, hoping that the twilight would shield us from outside observers.

Plato behaved like a well-trained police dog. Whether it was Lovely or Masters, Albert, Jeremiah or Vera who whistled his signal he paid attention and bolted for cover.

That night I wakened to the sounds of the hill – coyotes howling, grey foxes yapping, the mocking-bird's raucous 'sick-a-thee-thee-thee', the cat-like brawling of the racoons. It was such a noise that I could not be certain of hearing the barking of a dog in beween, but it seemed to me that there was a deeper voice mingling with the 'vow ya-ooo' of the coyotes.

I went back to sleep still wondering whether that sneaking fellow in the kilt had watched our work with Plato, whether Plato was being punished for what he had done.

The alsatian did not put in an appearance on the following day, and at night I again heard the strange voice among the coyotes.

This time I couldn't ignore it. I got up and dressed. Outside the moon was bright enough for me to see the path without stepping on a rattle-snake or the night-hunting California boa. But walking about that hillside was not comfortable; too many animals were preying on one another, too many tragedies were happening all around me. By the sound of it the coyotes were tearing apart some victim, the foxes were on the prowl and the swishing in the grass made me jump. I had not yet discovered how many poisonous snakes inhabited the estate. Towards the top of the hill, with the barking louder, I also had to beware of poison-ivy which could cause a skin-infection and high temperatures.

At the boundary of the estate the barking became distinctive. I no longer doubted that Plato was in trouble. The gentlemen of the *Decent Animals Federation* had erected a fence of high boards on their side. As I examined the new barrier the barking ceased, and I could hear a frenzied scratching and knocking. It sounded as if Plato was trying to uproot the boards.

While I stood there talking to the dog and trying to decide how best to help him Vera appeared, carrying a spade.

'That's swell,' she said. 'I wasn't sure I could get him on my own.'

'We shouldn't get him out at all.'

'Okay, if you're scared go back to bed.'

On the other side Plato was making little sounds of excitement and pleasure. 'All right, give me the shovel.'

We lifted our own wire-fence and I dug a hole under our neighbours' boards. Plato was so eager to get through that we had to dig him out with our hands.

We replaced the earth as best we could.

'Just the same,' said Vera, 'they'll know what we've done. But who cares!'

Certainly Plato cared. In the kitchen he finished off a large plate of meat and several bowls of water as if he'd been on hunger-strike.

'The rats!' Vera stroked Plato under the chin. 'They starved him.'

'He was probably too miserable to eat ... What are we going to do with him?'

'We are *not* taking him back.'

'You'll have a visit from Sam Bagshot tomorrow.'

'So what. Tomorrow Willard and Mother will be here.' Suddenly Vera appeared to me very young, neither assertive nor the provocative young woman who had made me feel hot under the collar. 'Mother will deal with Sam Bagshot ... She can send *anyone* up the flightdeck.'

The Duchess asked Jackie to have her fingernails cut so

as not to damage the morning papers in future, and then settled down to reading the report aloud.

'In brilliant sunshine four cars went to meet distinguished newly-weds at L.A. airport. The Duchess of Alanspring, formerly heiress Mrs Egon Miller-Hundling, was returning to one of her many homes with her husband, the English Duke of Alanspring. Accompanying them was the Duke's champion greyhound, Grey Rainbow.

'Meeting them were the Duchess's three English miniature terriers, Castor, Pollux and Manila, daughter Vera Miller-Hundling in a pair of pale blue silk trousers and matching shirt, Abdul Karim Kochbar – Grand Master of the Sisters of the Tibetan Truth and author of an animal-doctrine, the Grand Master's monkey Saint Cheetah and two good-looking young men so alike that I took them for brothers. In fact they were English and American vetinarians Michael Morton and Bertrand Hegel, joint-consultants with the Grand Master to the Duchess's new dog-training establishment, the *Wee Souls' Sanctuary Inc*.

'The Duchess may have expected this reception-gathering, but the occupants of the fourth car appeared to puzzle her. They were a Mr McCall, a gaunt kilted figure, who insisted on playing the bagpipes, and a jovial-looking businessman who turned out to be Mr Sam Bagshot jun., President of the *Decent Animals Federation*, owners of the estate adjoining the Duchess's residence in Santa Monica.

'The first intimation that all was not well came when Mr McCall's bagpipes startled the Duchess and the Duke offered the Scotsman a tip, which was indignantly rejected. Next Miss Miller-Hundling was seen conferring with her mother while the veterinarians and Abdul Karim Kochbar appeared to be conveying information to the Duke.

'When Mr Sam Bagshot approached the Duchess she thanked him for coming to welcome her, and led her party towards the elevator to the observation tower restaurant. Messrs Bagshot and McCall followed, protesting that they had serious matters to discuss.

'At the elevator the operator expressed his regret that Miss Miller-Hundling could not go up to the observation tower as there is a ruling that ladies in Capri-pants are barred from the bar and restaurant.

'The Duke protested against such "silly narrow-mindedness". Mr Bagshot said he was pleased there were places left where the decencies had to be observed; and thus the whole story came out.

'The *Decent Animals Federation* objects to the *Wee Souls' Sanctuary Inc.*, claiming that the Duchess of Alanspring's animals offend the sensibilities of its members as well as their animals. The Duchess and her veterinarians are opposed to putting clothes on their dogs, claiming that trews are unnatural and therefore cruel to the animals. Mr Bagshot further accused his neighbours of bodily abducting his alsatian Plato and of alienating the animal's natural affection.

'Miss Miller-Hundling and the veterinarians Morton and Hegel claimed that Plato had kept them awake "howling with misery" at night.

'This statement led to some polite but none the less serious differences of opinion, and Messrs Morton and Hegel had some difficulty in restraining Mr McCall from playing the bagpipes into the Duchess of Alanspring's ear. The Duke observed that his wife should not "trouble her head" about "a lot of cranks" and Mr Bagshot said he would consult his attorney.

'What does it all amount to? I say, it's a declaration of war. Since the fateful meeting at the airport Mr Bagshot has outlined his plans to me: his will be a two-pronged attack. On the one hand he will double the *Decent Animals Federation's* cash-allowance for enlightening literature, on the other he will prosecute anyone who interferes with D.A.F. animals or who undermines their morale by confronting them with unclothed animals.

'How does the Duke feel about the situation? He summed it up in one concise English word "balderdash". And the charming Duchess? "We're not interested in D.A.F.'s animals, but if they should come to us in distress we shall certainly not turn them away."'

The Duchess played with Plato's ear. 'Now isn't it nice ... all that free publicity for our training-school.'

'There's just as much publicity for our neighbours,' said

Rand.

'Lot of lunatics,' muttered the Duke. 'No one's going to pay attention to *them*.'

Rand still had his doubts. 'Perhaps we should do something positive.'

'Why, of course!' The Duchess pointed to a whole-page advertisement. 'We'll enter our dogs in the Los Angeles show ... my terriers and Grey Rainbow. That'll prove the *quality* of our animals. We could enter Plato as well.'

'Better not,' said the Duke.

'No,' agreed the Duchess, 'I guess we should buy him first.'

'You can try right now,' Vera pointed at the window, 'I think that's Sam Bagshot's car coming up the drive.' She whistled the *Stars and Stripes*; Plato leaped to attention and made for the terrace at the back of the house.

We all went to meet the President of D.A.F. Masters and Albert set out garden-chairs under a sycamore tree.

'It's real nice of you to call,' the Duchess welcomed Sam Bagshot. 'I just know if we get together...'

'Ma'am,' Sam looked extremely angry. 'If you just hand over my dogs, I'll go.'

'Your dogs?'

'My kennel-manager McCall has seen Plato here this morning.'

'With a pair of field-glasses?' asked Vera.

'We know Plato's here. There's also a poodle missing ... a male that answers to the name of Pip.'

'Mrs Gay Petrell's dog?' I asked.

'Ah, you know about it!'

'I saw her dogs in New York. But I didn't know they were here.'

'Pip *was* here until one of you removed him.'

'Look here,' said the Duke. 'You're talking rot, man. None of us *removed* your dogs. Something wrong, don't you think, if you can't keep them in order?'

'Let's have no arguments.' The Duchess put her hand on her husband's sleeve. 'Why don't you walk round with us, Mr Bagshot; then you'll see for yourself that we don't have any of your dogs.'

'I will,' said Sam. 'Sure I will.'

Things were almost cordial until we came to the gypsy-caravan folly; Sam Bagshot might have been convinced of our innocence if Abdul's monkey hadn't chosen that particular moment for tearing up a pair of pale blue stretch-nylon pants.

On the grass in front of the caravan Gipsy and Pip were behaving like a couple of lovers.

'Why, what do you know,' said the Duchess.

'Oh, I say,' said the Duke.

Sam Bagshot strode away. 'I'll see my attorney!'

Vera had to pick up Pip and run after him. 'Mr Bagshot, don't forget your dog!'

'How could he have gotten over that fence?' asked the Duchess.

'Obvious,' the Duke put his arm round her shoulders. 'That blasted monkey *lifted* him over ... I suppose old Pip was making a fuss on the other side. Nice little bitch, Gipsy.'

'I guess that guy won't sell us Plato now.'

'Don't suppose he will.'

'There's another problem,' Rand pointed out. 'Mrs Claude G. Blau may be kinda difficult if Gipsy has pups.'

CHAPTER EIGHT

Mrs Claude G. Blau junior gracefully accepted a cup of tea from the Duchess but ungraciously pointed out that she should have been consulted on the treatment of her poodle Gipsy. The Duchess, looking surprised, pointed out that Gipsy no longer bit her nails. Wasn't that the chief reason why Mrs Claude G. Blau had sent the little bitch to the *Wee Souls' Sanctuary*? Mrs Blau admitted she'd hoped Gipsy would be cured of that irritating habit but thought the treatment had been to drastic. Gipsy was too young to become a mother; besides, having puppies might spoil her figure.

The Duchess appealed to me; wasn't it true that a *young* bitch *wouldn't* lose her figure? I reassured Mrs Blau. I even suggested that Gipsy be entered in the pregnant bitches class at the L.A. dog-show; her condition was so good that she'd stand a good chance of winning her class. Mrs Blau consented.

We were hoping she would go in peace to supervise the packing for her world-tour, but she sat on until the Duke arrived. No doubt world-travellers were to be told what a distinguished-looking man the Duke was and how lucky Mrs Claude G. Blau had been to find a home for her poodle with those delightful Alansprings. I could see her build up the story while she was sipping her highballs, telling the Alansprings of the party she had given for Claude when he made his first million.

Masters had announced lunch for the third time before Mrs Blau accepted the fact that she was not being invited to stay, and rose to her plump little feet.

'It's been a real pleasure meeting you,' she said, shaking hands all round. 'And I guess Gipsy will come to no permanent harm owing to her ... ordeal. Of course you *will* make allowances for the ordeal, won't you? I guess if you redooce your fees from three hundred dollars a month to two hundred it's a deal.'

'Why, sure,' agreed the Duchess. 'Exclusive of veterinary treatment, of course, and the dog-show entry fee.'

The dog-show was my most valid reason for prolonging my stay in America. I had convinced myself that I couldn't go rushing home at this stage, but would I be able to convince Julia? Her letters had begun to show that my excuses were wearing thin.

She had inquired whether I'd finished my paper on Californian wild-life. She was aware of the curious prestige-value of publishing papers – matter of fact I just published a paper on the hairless black ear-rims of the hoary bat ... you know it, of course; the *lasiurus cinereus*. Extraordinary little creature if you think of it ... she approved of my diligence, but was I quite certain I was the right type for producing such academic gems?

Well, *was* I? Julia's doubts had hit the target. What was I doing about the hoary bat? Masters had put up a soft day-bed on the balcony outside my room, and there I was, lying in the sun, drinking iced orange-juice. Naturally, I was observing wild-life ... making mental notes.

A couple of minute green humming-birds (*calypte anna*) were assaulting the scarlet flowers of the cannas, their long beaks sucking the nectar with the greed of alcoholics. An ill-tempered bluejay kept diving at a stone under which a lizard was taking its siesta, and the little doe from up the hill had come looking for its precocious fawn.

Nothing there for a good solid academic paper. Could my night-observations be written up? There was the nasty hiss I got from a rattle-snake, or my discovery that the grey kit-foxes preferred chocolate biscuits to oatmeal cookies. Then there was the business of the racoons; away from human habitation it takes ten acres to feed one of these elegant little hunters with his black face-mask and ringed bushy tail. But on this hill there *was* human habitation, so human that the racoons thought nothing of visiting the kitchen in broad daylight. On one occasion, when Lovely had forgotten to put out the racoons' usual meal of bread, potatoes, meat and fruit, two racoons had walked into the

kitchen and helped themselves. They had opened the refrigerator, taken out of a jar of French salad-dressing, un-
screwed it and drained the contents.

No doubt a man with an academic turn of mind could at
least have produced a paper on the extraordinary adapta-
bility of the racoon's stomach, a paper proving that racoons
were highly intelligent stomachs with head, tail and fur
attachments – an academic exercise which would impress
the Royal College of Veterinary Surgeons. My trouble was
that I enjoyed the antics of animals too much to work up
the required standards of academic solemnity. And my
fiancée had always known it.

That left me the dog-show and – possibly – an inflated
account of the *Wee Souls' Sanctuary's* beginnings. Since the
Alansprings' arrival we had collected half a dozen assorted
puppies. There *were* things to be done, injections against
distemper and hardpad, house-training, obedience-training.
There was Plato, our not entirely ethical training-exhibit
number one, and then there were those delicate interviews
with policemen who had taken to nosing around in search
of stolen D.A.F. animals.

The exertion of composing my case for Julia sent me to
sleep until I heard a chime of cocktail-glasses and became
aware of Vera's hairdo tickling my face.

'Bloody Mary?' she crooned.

'Thanks.'

'What's the matter? You sound kinda grounded.'

'I am; and I should be up in the air, going home.'

'Crap. Rand and Abdul are still here.'

'Unnecessarily.'

'I don't know ... I guess Rand's staying because of me.
Well, I *won't* be possessed.'

'No fear of that. Rand's too busy possessing himself.'

'Maybe that's why I prefer you.' She put her arms round
my neck and gave me a kiss that got me up from the day-
bed. 'You *don't* possess yourself, do you Michael ... at least
not too much?'

'That's one good reason why I'd better go home.'

'And leave us here in trouble with Sam Bagshot and that
crazy McCall ... and the police?'

'Rand and Abdul can take care of that.'

'Abdul won't stay if you go. You *know* he's here because of you.'

'Nonsense.'

'Sure. He's homesick for England. He told me it's impossible to make friends here ... friends like the guys he used to know back home; and he *doesn't* mean India. While you're here he's having a ball.'

'All the same, our happy family will have to be broken up,' I told Vera.

'Not yet.' Vera poured me a Bloody Mary. 'We're going to Gay Petrell's wedding.'

'She hasn't been living in sin with her English water-power expert, has she?'

'Oh no, Clifford's a regular guy. It's her poodle Solly getting married to Rose of Sharon. The wedding's at the Miramar Hotel.'

'Who's dreamed this one up? The *Decent Animals Federation?*'

'No, it's Gay's idea. She rang up about it. Sam Bagshot *is* the best man, but she says he won't be there in his official capacity ... just as a friend of her dogs. She always gives a wedding-party when she mates one of them.'

'It's crazy.'

Vera laughed. 'Sure it's crazy. That's why I want to go.'

The french windows of the Hotel Miramar's ocean bar stood open to the swimming-pool. Some fifty guests were wandering about between the bar at one end of the room, the lily-decked miniature altar at the other and the pool-terrace where flood-lighting picked out a bank of pink and blue flowers.

I had hoped for a quiet talk with Sam Bagshot, an opportunity for making yet another offer for Plato. Since the alsatian couldn't be persuaded to go back to his master it didn't seem unreasonable of the Duchess to want to buy him. But, obviously, Sam was too preoccupied with his duties; one moment he was talking to McCall, who was wearing a cross between a surplice and an academic gown over his kilt, the next he was rushing about with the bridegroom under his arm. A lady in a handknitted dress and foxfurs whispered to us that the bridegroom was suffering from nerves and had been sick. She looked rather shocked when I pointed out that the most stolid of poodles might feel sick after being put into a black suit and a stiff white collar.

There was another hitch when a black cat came stalking into the bar. The bride, who wore a frilly white dress and a topknot of lilies of the valley, lost her composure, went racing after the cat, and had to be retrieved from the pool-terrace with her wedding-gown in disarray.

When the guests had almost forgotten the purpose of the party, enjoying the champagne, an electric organ suddenly sent a quiver through the bar. A master of ceremonies pleaded with us to divide, ladies on the right side of the room, gentlemen on the left. The organ droned sonorous chords until we were sorted out, and then broke into the 'Trumpet Voluntary'.

Solly, tail drooping under his black coat, and Rose of Sharon came padding down the aisle accompanied by Gay Petrell and Sam Bagshot. The little animals looked sleepy and slightly depressed.

'I guess they've been pumped full of tranquillizers,' said Rand, with disgust.

At the altar Solly tried to lie down but Sam firmly put him back on his feet.

McCall spread wide his arms, displaying gnarled knees and some kilt. 'Frriends,' he began, 'we're gatherred here farr a solemn occasion.'

No one seemed to mind that he somewhat mixed the marriage and the burial services, least of all the poor little poodles who had to be put back on their feet time and again. Instead of a ring the bride had a gold-chain put round her neck, and then the electric organ struck up the wedding-march. Bride and groom slunk through the aisle on to the terrace.

The guests clustered round as Sam Bagshot led the happy pair to the wedding-cake, a formidable white structure surmounted by a black poodle. Gay cut into it, serving a slice to bride and groom.

After some persuasion each animal sniffed at the cake. Rose of Sharon went so far as to take a lick, but Solly turned his head and was sick.

'I can't understand it,' said Gay. 'It's solid steak-hamburger and sour cream ... just what they like best.'

'Not today,' murmured Vera.

Gay abandoned the wedding-cake. 'Sam, I guess we'd better let them change.'

Sam Bagshot tucked bride and groom under his arms and took them away. The guests were served with the hamburger and more champagne. The women congratulated Gay ... such a cute party ... real moving ceremony ... the darlings, hadn't they been just too well-behaved?

I had noticed four women and a young man on the far side of the swimming-pool. The man, wearing nothing but a loincloth, and the women in curious baggy shifts did not look like wedding-guests. Suddenly several of the women around us screamed. The group across the pool had dropped their garments and were confronting our party split naked.

'It's a gimmick,' said Vera, angrily. 'Advertising the *Decent Animals Federation* ... showing us how awful nakedness can be.'

But apparently it was not a gimmick. Before anyone of our party understood what happened, a bunch of policemen came racing up to the naked group. They wrapped the struggling women in their shifts. But while they tried to carry them off the man had dived into the pool, quietly climbed out the other side and disappeared behind a shrubbery of flowering camellias.

The wedding-guests were too immersed in watching the strip-teasers being loaded into a van to notice their male companion appearing from the camellias dressed in an ordinary sober suit. He wandered in among us and accepted a glass of champagne a waiter had offered him.

He enthusiastically applauded with the guests when the bride and groom reappeared in a pink night-gown and blue silk pyjamas respectively.

One of the policemen came up to us, 'Seen a naked man?'

'No,' we said truthfully.

'Gee thanks.' The gatecrasher gave us a smile. 'You're swell.'

'Why did you do it?' asked Vera.

'We belong to the *Sons of Freedom*.'

'Yes, but why did you strip?'

'Oh, you don't know about us ... we're here on holiday, from Slocal Valley, Canada.'

'But who *are* you?'

'Never heard of the Doukhobors? ... Well, better come outside if you want me to tell you. Let's go to Zookie's. I like the food there.'

'Shouldn't you be doing something about your companions?' Vera was indignant. 'Get an attorney ... or something. They'll be in jail.'

'That's okay,' said the young man, politely stepping aside to let Vera walk out of the door first. 'My mother and sisters can take care of themselves. They're used to this kinda thing.'

'We didn't mean to strip while we're in the States,' explained Igor, spearing a piece of Zookie's special geffillte fish. 'But when we saw those little dogs all dressed up ...'

'I see what you mean,' said Vera. 'But why do you strip on other occasions?'

'To make God blush ... but it's more to keep the Mounties on the hop.'

'That a good thing?' asked Rand, doubtfully.

'Well, the Mounted Police are *authority*, aren't they?'

'So you don't believe in authority?'

'Or government ... man-made government,' said Igor. 'God is directly in every one of us, so what do we need governments for?'

'*I* sometimes wonder,' agreed Rand.

'There you are! My people oppose all authority, from schoolmasters to the prime minister. We've learned about human authority the hard way. In 1899 the Czar kicked us out of Russia and now the Communists won't let us go back to Russia.'

'So you stay in Canada and protest against authority by taking off your clothes.' Vera was looking thoughtful.

'We do more,' asserted Igor. 'We make bombs and blow up railroad lines, barns, crops.'

'Anything else?'

'Sure, sometimes we burn our own barns and crops ... even our cars.'

'What's the good of that?' I asked Igor.

'Obvious, isn't it? That's how the *Sons of Freedom* get new members. Know what it says about us in the new British Columbia Government study? It says "the satisfactions that life as a *Son of Freedom* can provide are many for people who need to express hostility, to protest and destroy, to suffer, to atone for guilt".'

'That's great!' Vera suddenly looked like the Duchess when she'd suggested entering Plato in the dog-show. 'I can see now why you just had to strip when you saw these poodles all dressed up.'

'You can?' Igor seemed pleased to have found such understanding.

'Sure I can. What could be more like authority ... not only making people wear a kinda uniform ... but putting *animal*s in clothes. It made you sick, didn't it?'

'Sure.'

'You should *tell* the public why you stripped, shouldn't you?'

'I guess so.'

'Listen Igor, it's easy. All you got to do is ring up a newspaper and tell them you protested against the *Decent Animals Federation*.'

'Who are they?'

'Gee, the people who're trying to get animals put in clothes. Will you do it?'

'I reckon that *would* be protesting against authority?'

'Why, what else?'

Around midnight we drove Igor back to his hotel where his mother and sisters had reached the point of requesting the police to search for him.

On the way home I told Vera that she shouldn't have made use of these people.

'Why not? It was just what we needed ... a public protest against Sam Bagshot's crap.'

'It wasn't playing the game.'

'Oh, you English! You didn't even get Sam to sell us Plato. And tomorrow's the last day we can enter him in the show.'

CHAPTER NINE

'It's himm.' McCall opened the door to an office.

'Who?' asked Sam Bagshot.

'Himm, from the other side.' The Scotsman made it sound as if he'd just found a rattle-snake from hell.

'Come in,' said Sam. He was sitting at his desk, head in hands, staring at a pile of newspapers. 'Sit down, Mr Morton ... I guess you've seen the ... er, publicity.'

'Well, yes. But I haven't come...'

'No decency,' said Sam, sadly. 'It's downright irresponsible how our papers have inflated the ... incident. It isn't as if Mrs Petrell had invited these lunatics to the wedding. They shouldn't have come if they don't appreciate properly dressed animals. And to make a public protest! The papers should never have printed it. Foreigners they are ... not even American citizens! It was a real pretty wedding too.'

'It was rather unfair.' I was thinking of the part Vera had played in getting the 'incident' publicized. 'Even if one doesn't agree with your ideas...'

'Aye.' McCall had remained on guard at the door. 'Ye'll no get any sympathy from himm, Mr Bagshot.'

'I *am* sorry.' I meant that. Sam's sadly sentimental mood was worse than his aggressiveness because it was touching.

'Why, thanks, Mr Morton. It was friendly of you to call.'

'I wanted to have a word with you about Plato.' I told him. 'Whether or not you believe me we had no intention of getting Plato away from you. We simply can't keep the dog out. In the circumstances wouldn't it be easier all round if you sold the animal to us? The Duchess of Alanspring is prepared to pay your price.'

'I guess you have an argument. Well, tell the lady I'll give consideration to her offer.'

'She was hoping we might settle the business now.'

McCall strode up to the desk. 'Aye, yon woman wants the dog. And I ken fine why. They've enterred their animals in the L.A. dog-show.'

'Why not?' It occurred to me that my fellow Scots at their angriest were first-rate haters.

'I'll tell ye, Mr Bagshot ... They want to display *our* dog too. Aye, and show him *naked*.' McCall hovered about Sam's chair, the perfect *éminence grise*. 'Ye can tell your mistress we're showing Plato ourselves ... in a pair of decent trews.'

'Are we?' Sam looked at his kennel manager, and then at me. 'Why yes, that's right ... We're not selling an animal of ours to be displayed in a state of indecency.'

'Mr Bagshot,' I appealed, 'you may not be *able* to show Plato. The judges won't give an opinion on a covered-up dog ... unless this show is run by extraordinary rules.'

'It will be,' said McCall. 'We can make a request for a special class.'

'I guess that's our decision.' Sam got up. 'McCall, where *is* Plato?'

'That's what I was coming to see ye aboot. I canna find yon dog any place.'

Sam turned on me. 'He's at *The Cottage* again, isn't he?'

'I haven't seen him this morning,' I said, truthfully.

'If that is so, I guess you won't mind Mr McCall going to your place right now.'

'Of course not.'

'In your car.'

There was no way of warning my friends. And, of course, no one paid any attention to Rand's car turning into the drive. Pretending that the engine had died on me I left the car by the gate and made McCall walk up to the house. It was no use. Vera, Rand and Abdul were sitting on the lawn studying the kennel-club rules; Plato was lying under the table, his tail and hindquarters plainly visible.

'So ye dinna ken where the dog is,' said McCall.

If any of us had given Plato's whistle, making him run for cover, it would have ruined the dog's future chances of escape. We all realized it, and kept quiet. McCall grabbed the dog's legs and dragged him out. Plato twisted and growled, but McCall had come well equipped. With amazing speed he took a muzzle from his sporran. Controlling the dog with his sharp knees he put it on, and then fixed a metal-studded collar and lead.

The dog pulling at his arm, he gave us a sour stare. 'Ye won't be troubled with himm any more, I warrant ye. And don't ye try any of your tricks or I'll have the police on ye for stealing.'

Plato dug in his feet, but the Scotsman was stronger. He dragged the alsatian down the drive, occasionally giving the collar a vicious tug. As long as he could see us Plato kept turning round, his eyes puzzled and unhappy.

'He won't trust *anyone* now,' said Vera.

We had planned to go swimming; instead, without saying anything, we all spent the afternoon in the garden. Any movement in the bushes made us jump, and when Grey Rainbow came streaking down the hill Vera ignored his overtures.

After dinner she could stand it no longer. 'Let's go out.'

'Where?' asked Rand.

'Why don't you produce an original idea?'

'There's a movie ...'

'Crap. It's too warm for the movies. And *don't* tell me the theatres are air-conditioned,' she flared at him.

'Okay, where do you want to go?'

'Oh, anywhere.'

'La Cienega,' suggested Abdul. 'If Michael hasn't been there he'll find it rather fascinating, don't you think?'

'It's as good as any other place.'

As we reached the cross-roads with the *Decent Animals Federation* signpost we heard what might have been Plato's bark, and Vera burst into tears. 'Gee, I'm sorry ... but when I think of this beautiful dog...'

We were still thinking of Plato when Rand parked the car in an avenue of small individual villas. Strolling along towards a more brightly-lit road we passed a restaurant which advertised 'The world's greatest entertainer, come in, get lost', and a big shop-window displaying a swimming-pool with live people in it. At the side of the pool an elderly woman with astounding muscles was lifting weights.

The main street of La Cienega, yet another district of

omnivorous Los Angeles, looked like the most charming and well-manicured parts of Chelsea. The antique-shops displayed originality, good taste and *joie de vivre*; colours of moss-green, white and orange in a drawing-room corner – mixed blues and green as a background for a Meissen dinner-service – an Italian inlay table shown against a bank of scarlet cannas.

A few blocks down there was a village of art-galleries, some open to the lawns of the sidewalk, some tucked away among palm-trees, miniature flower gardens and sculptures.

At the entrance to Esther-Robles's gallery we came upon a bronze sculpture by Paul Granlund called 'gordian figure II', a female figure reclining on one buttock with its arms and legs intertwined like a grapevine.

'Does it give you that psychological feeling?' I asked Vera.

She gave me a watery smile. 'Not as much as usual. Let's go in.'

Granlund's 'Jacob and the angel' and 'horizontal lovers II' were equally successful in refuting the laws of gravity and physiology. A boy in paint-smeared jeans and black shirt was lying in the centre of the floor trying to prove to his girl-friend that one *could* balance on one shoulder-blade and one ear. After several collapses he became rather cross and accused her of being no help to a man.

Abdul disappeared into the Gallery's office; when he rejoined us he looked pleased with himself. 'Absolutely perfect, "Jacob and the angel", don't you think? Bought it for my *Self-knowledge* show. You know, the temple of the *Sisters of the Tibetan Truth*.'

'It's not Tibetan, is it?' asked Rand.

'That's just the point, old man ... Esther-Robles wants us to have a drink with her.'

We were offered sherry in a little room at the back of the gallery; we listened to Esther-Robles's plans for exhibiting the paintings of the Spanish artist Tharrats, and confirmed her opinion that Tharrats was a little unwise in the choice of titles for his pictures. A title such as *El cel va des-aparèixer com un full que s'enrotlla, i totes les muntanyes i les illes varen moure's del seu lloc*, poetic though it was, would probably elude the memories of prospective buyers. Artists were somewhat difficult, Esther observed, accepting Abdul's cheque.

The Ryder Gallery next door was showing pottery-sculptures by Bertil Valien, a young Swede who gave machine-shapes human character and vice versa. Here was a formidable talent for creating petrified nightmares, yet some of his pieces possessed a sense of humour.

'What do you know?' said a wondering voice behind us. It belonged to a man who didn't seem to know what to do with his hands. He looked incomplete without a bundle of progress-reports or balance-sheets.

'It's handsome.' His wife touched a piece that looked like a couple of kids having a free ride on a bus. 'I think this is a real sensitive pot, George.'

'Wanta buy?'

'Well ... the King of Sweden's got one just like it.'

Higher up La Cienega Boulevard the Ankrum and Ceejé galleries were busy selling the paintings of Morris Broderson – a yellow boy clasping a yellow tree in front of a yellow wall, or seated figures against a background of machinery which also looked like seated figures. Someone gave us goblets of wine.

'I dunno,' muttered a blond, hairy young man. 'I think Calliope does this sort of thing better, don't you?'

'Sure,' agreed his equally hairy companion. 'But Broderson's related to the owners of the gallery ... It's the only way to make these people sell your work ... marry a gallery.'

At the Comara gallery they were showing Jack Hopkins's jewellery, strange lumps of silver or gold incorporating stranger lumps of obsidian, malachite or quartz. Vera said they'd look good on a dead plain dress. We each took a catalogue and received a glass of beer.

We wandered on between lawns and brightly lit windows, among dozens of art-lovers enjoying the warm night.

'Now there'sh shculpture,' said a man, standing with his nose pressed flat against a window. 'Besht I've seen, Betty.'

Betty successfully prevented him from toppling over. 'Come along, Henry ... You're high, boy.'

' 'M not ... Great, real great shculpture, n'all pink ... pink,' he asserted, pointing at the beauty parlour which was displaying the latest in hair-driers.

Vera giggled. 'I guess I've had enough to drink ... let's just go into one more gallery. How about the Landau?'

The Landau was showing the most uncompromising paintings I'd ever seen – by a Japanese artist; a stark black canvas with a single yellow line down the middle and a picture which looked like a chunk of crumbling plaster with a black dot in the top right-hand corner.

Vera screwed up her face. 'I kinda like this.'

'Why?' I asked.

'It's got something ... Oh, Michael! You won't see it like *this* ... with your eyes wide open.' Hers screwed up to slits. 'You've gotta put your eyes at half-mast.'

'Well, I see spots.'

'*There*, you're with it now.'

On our way back to the car Abdul suddenly stopped and stared at the first-floor windows of a gallery which appeared to have no name. 'John O'Neils,' he said, gazing reverently at the half-dozen abstract paintings.

The pictures deserved his admiration. Each one, a masterpiece of colours and textures, celebrated the miracles of light. I thought even the most sceptical enemy of abstract art would admit that John O'Neil was a great artist.

'He's worth all the rest put together,' said Abdul. 'The only abstract painter whose work I want to buy.'

'Me too,' agreed Rand.

'Why don't you?' I asked.

'It's kinda hard talking business with him,' explained Vera. 'He's too interested in painting.'

'You can buy a painting from his gallery.'

'Not a chance,' said Abdul. 'When O'Neil has a show his friends get to know about it.'

'Don't other painters tell their friends when they're having shows?' I asked.

'Certainly, but they're *not* O'Neil.'

'The galleries must make a living just the same.' I had been genuinely impressed by the amount and variety of art in La Cienega.

'Sure,' said Rand. 'A lot of interior decorating firms do their buying here. The clients ask them to furnish a home, and that's what they do; they put in everything from wash-basin's to paintings.'

'Home?' asked Rand, as we piled into his car.

'No.' Vera sounded depressed again.

'Ice-cream?'

'I guess not ... Gee, I don't want to go back just yet. If I heard Plato bark ...'

Abdul looked at his watch. 'Nearly midnight ... Perhaps you'd like to go to Venice. I have some new twist-records at my place ... Think there's enough vodka. We could pick up May ... Oh Lord! May's doing the mysteries tonight. I forgot. If you like ...'

'Take us to the mysteries,' said Vera. 'That *would* be something.'

'I say!' Surprisingly, the framer of doctrines looked some-what embarrassed. 'You know, I don't think you'd enjoy it ... Actually it's for members only.'

'But you're the Grand Master.'

'That's another word for administrator. I really don't think ...'

'Don't think; let's go,' said Vera.

'If you wish. But you'll have to sit behind the screen. May's frightfully good, but the moment she sees an outside-observer she bungles the telephone-rites.'

In moonlight the whole of Venice had the appearance of a ritual domain. The oil-pumps not only looked like ob-scene grasshoppers but like grasshoppers bewitched by the curse of perpetual motion. The hamburger stalls and Coca-Cola bars were closed, but in a discotheque on the beach a handful of juveniles were dancing – eyes vacant, faces grim, bodies swinging like puppets abandoned to a backstage draft.

'On Monday nights Venice is pretty dead,' apologized Abdul. But even on a Monday eternal life was being catered for; the temples and the churches, mosques and synagogues produced a wilderness of neon-lights.

The *Temple of Self-knowledge*, tucked away among its palm-trees, was floodlit – which seemed to confuse the fish in the pond. Whenever a mosquito-fish leaped out of the water the reflection of the temple became unsteady, emitting eerie little eels of light.

'Oh Lord!' Abdul hesitated at the entrance, 'May's started her show. Better come round the back.'

He led us through a 'vestry' which contained a closet full of brightly-coloured saris and cloaks, a large dressing-table crammed with grease-paint, lipsticks and other beauty-preparations, and a stand with Mattie's cage. Beyond the vestry there was a narrow passage with a few chairs and about fifteen feet of carved oriental screen.

Through the screen we could see the temple proper. About fifty women in filmy harem-trousers, tight jackets and feathered head-dresses were sitting on cushions on the floor, forming a circle round a shallow copper-bowl which May was feeding with aromatic herbs.

After several minutes' silence lights went on above her head and some kaleidoscopic device shed moving patterns of gold and purple, green and blue over her white cloak. The restless flickering gave May an appearance of disembodied grace.

With a slow movement she produced Mattie the hamster out of her wide sleeve. 'Behold the sign of self-knowledge!' Mattie, on May's outstretched hand, sat up and began to eat a nut or a biscuit.

'This little mouse,' said May, 'is the humblest creature on earth. Let him remind you, Sisters of the Tibetan Truth, that only the humblest among you can attain true knowledge of self which is a state of happiness.'

She grabbed Mattie and his food and returned them to the inside of her sleeve. 'It is the Merciful who is teaching you,' she began in a liturgical voice. 'The Lord of the two easts is He, and the Lord of the two wests. Which of your Lord's blessings would you deny?'

'The Koran,' murmured Abdul.

'He has let loose the two oceans: they meet one another. Yet between them stands a barrier which they cannot overrun. Which of your Lord's blessings would you deny?'

All movement among the women had ceased. They were gazing at May in her mantle of flashing lights.

'Mankind and jinn, if you have power to penetrate the confines of heaven and earth, then penetrate them!' May's command met with a silence in which one could hear the small explosions of the burning herbs. 'Sisters, the Truth is among you!' May threw wide her right arm, 'And those of you who acknowledge it shall go to heaven.' The lining of the cloak billowed out sky-blue. 'And those who do not acknowledge it shall go to hell.' May flung out her left arm revealing a panel of flame-red silk. 'The Truth is among you.'

A bell beside May began to ring. She turned, revealing the pillar-fragment against which she had been leaning. The antique wall-telephone, fixed to its scrolls, gleamed like a jewel.

'The Truth is among us,' said May, picking up the mink-covered receiver. 'You are to begin, Sisters.' She casually replaced the instrument.

One of the old ladies prostrated herself, the feathers of her turban touching the ground. 'The Truth revealed itself to me,' she said.

'How?' asked May.

'You remember when we had the last Mysteries, honey ... our priestess? Well, I got a kinda message I'd have a car-smash if I went home along Sunset Boulevard.'

'What happened?'

'I went home through Westwood, and I *didn't* have a car-smash. The Truth saved my life.'

'Why, isn't that wonderful!' exclaimed her neighbour.

'Well, *I* don't think that was the Truth,' said a woman behind them.

'Dottie Millington!' the woman who'd had the revelation sounded indignant. 'If you can't see it was the Truth saved my life you shouldn't be here.'

The telephone rang. 'The Truth,' said May, 'is disgusted with Dottie for doubting our Sister Angela.'

Dottie subsided.

'The Truth revealed itself to me,' announced a woman on the far side of the circle. 'I've been married to Edgar thirty-one years, and yesterday the Truth suddenly kinda hit me. I don't like the guy. I wish he was dead. I really do.'

'Sister Evelyn, I declare!' The outraged person was younger than the rest. 'Maybe it isn't like that at all. Maybe your stomach was upset.'

'Sister, when my stomach's upset I don't give a thought to Edgar. I just know it was the Truth,' insisted Evelyn.

The telephone rang again. This time May listened longer than usual. 'Sister Evelyn,' she put down the receiver very slowly. 'I hear you may be misguided by a spirit of hell.' Her left arm shot out, revealing the red lining. 'You are to seek more deeply, and reveal yourself again at our next Mysteries in three weeks' time.'

'I say!' Abdul looked pleased. 'Well done, don't you think? Rather tricky, this sort of situation.'

Sister Evelyn's confession was followed by others which were less dramatic. Sister Paula acknowledged the fact that she became chairman of a children's committee not because she cared about the kids but to ensure that Mrs Shuster didn't get the job. Sister Mary had discovered that she watched westerns on television because she enjoyed seeing people get killed, and Sister Wendy admitted coveting her daughter's boy-friend.

When a lull in the Truth-seeing set in, a red light inside the copper-bowl began to flash and the herbs sent up a thick column of smoke. May, slow and queenly, stepped inside. 'Sisters, you've passed the eucalyptus-test real well. In three weeks' time you'll be privileged to pass on to the sycamore-test.'

Abdul's monkey, who had slept most of the evening, suddenly became excited. He jumped down from his chair and made off, reappearing among the Sisters.

May, catching him in her arms, imperturbably wound up the ceremony. 'The wrong-doers shall be known by their looks,' she recited. A distant chanting began to accompany her voice. 'They shall be seized by their forelocks and their feet. Which of your Lord's blessings would you deny?'

The bowl with May in its centre slowly lowered itself to the floor. As the chanting became louder May began to disappear downward, and finally a silent panel slid across her exit. Only the pillar with the antique telephone remained. The Sisters rose to their feet; little boys in long white gowns and yellow turbans offered them cookies and Coca-Cola, for which they paid.

May, with Saint Cheetah in her arms, came in from the 'vestry'. 'Gee, why didn't you tell me you were watching?' she greeted us.

Abdul patted her shoulder, 'Don't worry, my dear, you were perfectly splendid. Wasn't she?'

We all agreed.

'That's real kind of you,' said May. 'But if I'd known you were here I wouldn't have used the telephone ... It's more difficult, but I *can* do without ... Wasn't Dottie Millington awful? You know, about Sister Angela's car-smash revelation. Dottie's kinda jealous every time one of the girls gets a hold of a good truth.'

'Forget about it,' said Abdul. 'You're not on duty now. Put on a dress. I've got some new records.'

'Great! I need some exercise.' May slipped off her cloak. 'Gee! Mattie's eaten a hole in my sleeve again.'

'Perhaps you could do without Mattie now.'

'Oh no! He's great for the opening-scene.'

'I dare say we could work out an opening with Saint Cheetah.'

'With that monkey?'

That monkey was quite docile while we danced to jive music, but when Abdul put on his records Saint Cheetah intervened. When she failed in stripping off Vera's skirt she got to work on Rand, almost debagging him. Since neither May nor Abdul thought of putting Saint Cheetah into her cage we soon stopped dancing.

'Wonder what bothers her about dancing.' Abdul poured us glasses of his appalling concoction – vodka, tonic-water and lime-juice, the latest Californian cocktail.

'It's the movement Saint Cheetah doesn't like,' said Vera. 'I've noticed it before.'

Abdul nodded. 'That would explain how the poodle lost his trousers ... the D.A.F. poodle who mated with Mrs Blau's bitch.'

'Sure,' said Vera. 'We caught her with the pants in her teeth.'

'That doesn't mean Saint Cheetah actually took them off.'

'I guess she did.'

'Suppose so.'

Perhaps we were getting tired or perhaps the vodka had a depressing effect, but suddenly everyone became rather silent and torpid. May put on a disc of Burl Ives singing his most gruesome railroad song, 'Gotta-aa die on this goddam blue mo-orning ... Gotta-aa die on this endless damned line ...'

'Alienated,' murmured Vera. 'Dr Bonblust says we're all alienated.'

'What's it mean?' asked May, lifting her head from Abdul's shoulder.

'I guess it means you don't connect.'

'*I* connect.'

'You only think you do.'

'Abdul,' May subsided again, 'don't I connect?'

'Well ... better than most people ... Put on another record, dear.'

'Cabaret?'

'Too bouncy,' said Vera. 'Another Burl Ives.'

'Does he give you that psychological feeling?' I asked.

Vera left my side and went to sit beside Rand. '*You* don't get psychological feelings,' she said, bitterly.

'I've got one now,' I told her.

'What kind?'

'The kind that tells me I should stop drinking vodka and go home or I won't be fit for the dog-show tomorrow.'

'Corny.'

We had more silence, more Burl Ives and more vodka. I said I thought Russians and Californians had something in common – especially the gloom. Rand said he knew that was true; he'd known a Russian who worked on a farm and got drunk and morose every night. But one night he started reminiscing. He told the people in a bar how he'd seen a man drown in the Volga; and then he began to laugh, and nobody could stop him laughing, and then he gasped for air and fell down dead.

At dawn, with Saint Cheetah obstructing me as best she could, I made black coffee, which infused enough vitality into our party to put us back on the road.

Saint Cheetah went to sleep on my lap, Vera on Rand's shoulder. The crazy grasshoppers of Venice were still pumping up and down. On the beach a few sleepers-out were picking themselves up, avoiding the penalties for *being* picked up. The bells of a Catholic church were ringing matins.

The entrance to a grand, ultra-modern business-block was being decorated with flowers and banners announcing the dog-show. Abdul assured me it was no mistake; progressive banks were only too pleased to lend their premises for fashion or dog-shows. It gave them that human touch which was so good for business.

CHAPTER TEN

'Got the blighter!' The Duke, gun in the crook of his arm, appeared on the terrace. He held up by the ears a puny dead rabbit. 'Rotten luck Grey Rainbow having a scare ... today of all days.'

'He's getting over it,' I told him.

'Stopped shivering, has he?'

'Just about.'

'Better keep an eye on him until we're ready to go, in case another rabbit pops up under his nose.'

Masters came out of the kitchen. 'Sir, Grey Rainbow's bath is ready.'

'Get on with it then.'

'Sir, Lovely ... Mrs Albert wouldn't let me use the sink, so I've taken the French hip-bath from the flower-room.'

'Oh, Willard!' The Duchess let go Manila, who had not enjoyed being brushed and took the opportunity of bolting into the bushes. 'You're *not* bathing the dog in the kitchen, are you?'

'Why not, dear?'

'It's so unhygienic.'

'Nonsense, Sonia. Always used to give Grey Rainbow his bath in the kitchen at Hazelbridge House.' The Duke omitted to mention that the *Northwing*'s 'kitchen' had been the only living-room and that the house had been too ancient for conveniences such as a bathroom. 'Dog's perfectly clean,' he added.

'If you say so.' The Duchess looked half-convinced. 'What are you going to wear?'

'Suit that fellow Gluckstein made for me, I suppose.'

'Too formal ... with your dog. A greyhound's a sporting dog, honey. Why don't you wear your Norfolk jacket?'

'Thought you didn't care for it.'

'Not at a cocktail-party, honey. But I think it'll look real nice today. How old did you say it was?'

'Got to work it out ... Grandfather had it made in 1875, just after Gladstone resigned. Then my Uncle Charles got it ... let me see ... during Queen Victoria's jubilee, yes, that was in 1887. My father borrowed it the year Lord Kitchener drowned ... 1916, wasn't it? Anyway I know he got Harborows to remodel it in 1925, the day Madame Tussaud's burnt down.'

'I sure wish I had your memory.' The Duchess's eyes were warm with admiration. 'The Norfolk jacket won't be too warm for you?'

'Always feel comfortable in it.'

'There's just no country outside United Kingdom that makes such indestructible cloth. That's why Gluckstein won't use any other. Do *you* know, Michael,' she turned to me, 'Gluckstein won't touch Terylene, though it loses him a big summer trade.'

'With the prices he charges,' said the Duke, 'he doesn't have to work in summer. Fellow told me he's got an estate in Florida ... breeds Dobermans ... beastly German police dogs.'

'Manila!' The Duchess had caught sight of her little terrier savaging a plastic dish. She seemed to have chewed off the rim.

I went to separate Manila and the dish.

'Will she be sick?' the Duchess prodded the animal's stomach. 'If she disgraces herself at the show...'

I thought Manila looked pleased with herself. 'Perhaps we should give her something to make her sick *now* ... I'll ask Rand. He knows more about dog-shows.'

I found Rand at the caravan with Gipsy. 'Funny, the way everything goes wrong before a dog-show,' he said.

'What's the matter with her?'

'I guess she's upset because she can hear Pip over at the D.A.F. place, and he isn't coming to her. She's been biting her nails again. Look,' he held out a paw for my inspection.

'It's all right.'

'Well, I've cut the nails as best I can. But the judges might notice how short they are.'

'Shouldn't think so. They look even.' I sat down on the

steps beside him. 'Manila's been eating plastic dog-plates.'

'Yeah ... It's always the the same before a show.' He stared in front of him. 'I guess you'll quit as soon as it's over.'

'I should have gone home weeks ago. Julia's getting impatient.'

'Julia?'

'Girl I'd have married by now if she hadn't gone down with appendicitis.'

'Does Vera know you're engaged? ... It wouldn't make any difference to her though. Engagements can be broken, can't they?'

'Nonsense, Vera isn't interested in me.'

'Are you sure?' Rand sounded almost happy.

'Positive.'

'She isn't interested in me either.' Rand returned to his morose contemplation of the middle-distance. 'Anyway, why *should* she want to marry a veterinarian?'

'She's fond of animals.'

'Sure.'

'Have you asked her to marry you?'

'We talked about getting engaged when she was still at college. I thought she kinda liked me. But after she went to New York she changed. Other fellows around, I suppose ... fellows like you.'

'I was just a novelty.'

'You don't bore her.'

'Neither do you, Rand ... except when you're being morose.'

'Well, I get depressed because she keeps changing; one moment she behaves as if I'd been her boy-friend all along, next moment I'm just a drip who's spoiling the party.'

'Vera's a spoilt brat.'

'But you think she's attractive, don't you?'

'Well ... yes.'

'That's the trouble. No one can get mad at her.'

'Maybe that's what you should do ... get mad at her.'

'What for?'

'Rand!' Vera came up the path with Grey Rainbow on a lead. 'Rand, have you finished Gipsy's nails? Don't be all day about it!'

'Okay. Gipsy's ready.'

'You should have told her to go to hell,' I said.

'Why, she'd be hurt.'

Vera, in a white suit, hair gleaming in the sun, looked charming. She planted herself in front of Rand. 'Aren't you going to change?'

'There's plenty of time.'

'You'll make us late ... better have a shave too.'

'I *am* shaved.'

'You want to get yourself a new razor, or a lawn-mower.'

Rand got up, and walked off towards the house.

'You shouldn't bully people,' I told her.

'Well, what can you do with a guy like that?' She rubbed her nose against my cheek. 'I feel like making love.'

'Last night you were making love to Rand.'

'It didn't get me any place, did it?'

'Did you want it to?'

Vera thought for a while. 'I guess not; not as long as Rand would feel guilty afterwards. *You* wouldn't feel guilty, would you?'

'Better not try me.'

'I've been thinking about it. Maybe Rand's right about one thing. The way things are when you're at college you kinda get used to necking, and some guys get caught young. Girls too.'

'You're out of college now.'

'I know. But some of my friends got married and it didn't work out, and some didn't get married and they keep going from one guy to another. Looks like you just can't win ... I get scared. What I want is a man who doesn't really want to have sex but ... well, I suppose someone who just makes it happen.'

The perfume of her hair under my nose got too much. 'Nothing's going to happen *now*,' I told Vera, 'because it's almost dog-show time, and your stepfather's looking for us.'

The Duke's elongated Norfolk jacket almost covered his breeches. He looked unmistakably English until one became aware of his shoes, a pair of white buckskins with brown toe-caps.

'Isn't he cute?' whispered Vera.

'Blasted shindy!' said the Duke, one hand at his ear. 'Hear it?' There was a faint sound of bagpipes from the top of the hill. Apparently the dogs of the *Decent Animals Federation* were being piped off their premises. 'Look sharp, Vera, your mother wants to get to the show before *they* do.'

CHAPTER ELEVEN

'What did you say your name was?' The registration clerk looked up at the Duke.

'Alanspring.'

'Initials?'

'W.H.G. ... Duke of.'

The clerk looked irritated; the sun was burning through the plate-glass windows and the wilting flowers made the office stuffy. The air-conditioning didn't seem to work as it should. The clerk slipped on a pair of sun-glasses. 'Dook-of ... how do you spell it.'

'Why it's not difficult at all,' said the Duchess. 'Now, you've seen me in this bank before, haven't you?'

'Yes, ma'am. But we aren't open for business today.'

'No, you're having a dog-show. Listen! I am the Duchess of Alanspring, and this is my husband, the Duke of Alanspring.'

'Sorry, ma'am, no foreign entries.'

While the Duchess explained to the clerk that she and the Duke were residents in America and accepted his apologies a man with a movie-camera took pictures of Grey Rainbow, Gipsy and our three miniature terriers.

'You the Duke's kennel-men?' he asked.

'Are you a reporter?' asked Vera.

'Television,' the man answered, meekly. 'I'm Ben Dryer.'

Vera introduced Rand and me as the Alansprings' veterinarians, Abdul as an adviser and Saint Cheetah as our mascot. Ben, much impressed with our 'high-power' team, said he had television cameras in the show-hall and he hoped to get some good shots of us.

Sam Bagshot and McCall watched our talk with Ben Dryer rather balefully. Sam, in a light suit, looked as much as ever an energetic businessman but McCall, in tweeds, cut an insignificant figure. Without his kilt his fierceness appeared pathetic. His bagpipe-arm, giving oddly unco-ordinated twitches and jerks, betrayed the unease of the man. Both Sam and McCall wore the badges of the *Decent Animals Federation* which incorporated the crest – two dogs rampant in military cloaks supporting their sword-bearing musclebound knight.

Ben Dryer took some pictures of the D.A.F. animals, of Plato in a pair of dark green trews, Pip in sober grey and a couple of dachshunds in scarlet pants. Pip had strained at his lead and cried ever since he'd discovered Gipsy in the crowd, but Plato was unnaturally quiet and distant. I felt sure he'd been given a tranquillizer.

'Crazy lot.' Ben Dryer shook his head. 'Didn't some Canadians demonstrate against animals wearing clothes ... a short while ago?'

'Sure,' Vera said, calmly. 'We saw it.'

'What happened?'

'Someone arranged a wedding for a couple of poodles ... you know ... wedding-dress, religious service, cake ... just everything. It made the Canadian guests real sick, so they took their clothes off ...'

'*All* their clothes?'

'Yes. They wanted to prove that naked people didn't look half as bad as dressed-up dogs.'

'Would you say they made their point?'

'Of course they did, or the newspapers wouldn't have taken it up.'

'Your family's against putting animals in clothes?'

'Definitely. It's cruel.'

Ben looked at Vera – wishfully, I thought. 'Miss Miller-Hundling, would you say there's a chance of a demonstration against D.A.F. at this show?'

The official veterinary surgeon, knowing Rand, gave our dogs no more than a cursory examination. His assistant stamped their chits and told us to go right in. Abdul left Saint Cheetah in charge of an attendant whose job it was to look after non-competing pets.

The main hall was already lively with animal-owners nervously brushing their dogs and dogs who, according to their masters, behaved unusually badly. The owners had

dressed in styles that were meant to live up to the per-
fection of their animals. Poodle-owners tended towards
fluffy hats, spaniel-fanciers, setter and gundog-owners went
in for tweeds and brogues, the terrier-varieties appeared to
demand tailored town-styles, while boxers and alsations
went mostly with young men in dark shirts.

'Isn't the antiseptic smell awful?' said Vera.

'You're pale, honey.' The Duchess gave her daughter an
appraising look. 'You're not going to be sick, are you?'

'No ... but I wish we'd taken oranges.'

'I'll get you some,' I offered.

'Thanks, Michael. I guess the nearest place is the supermarket, back of the bank.'

Outside, in the asphalt-heat, it occurred to me that I had
seen nothing but supermarkets in the Los Angeles area – no
greengrocers, butchers, bakers. I had bought my cigarettes
or tobacco from machines and I'd done no other shopping.

The supermarket's doors, controlled by a photo-electric
cell, opened before me like gates to a cool sesame. The soft
music was syncopated by the clicking of cash-registers, but
there were no recognizable human sounds. Even the metal
trolleys the customers were filling with their purchases
lacked the friendly squeaks and creaks that engender a
sense of familiarity with a mechanical device.

I walked through aisle after aisle of pickles, jams, cookies,
all brightly labelled. Ingeniously the canned fruits were
placed beside cream, meats beside spaghetti or rice. A scat-
tering of coffee on the floor provided an appetising scent;
bins with somewhat untidily arranged cut-price goods gave
certain corners a 'homey' atmosphere.

One of those bins reminded me that I wanted a tube of
shaving-cream. I bent down and helped myself, wondering
why shaving-cream should be less conveniently placed than
other goods. I soon discovered the answer. As I straightened
up I was faced by a row of expensive French perfumes,
luxuries a man was *meant* to notice.

As it happened it did occur to me that Vera – beset by
smells of dog and antiseptic – might appreciate another
scent, so I took a bottle of *Miss Dior*. I passed refrigerators
displaying fish, meats, cheeses and vegetables, but there was

no sign of oranges. Certain I'd find fruit *somewhere* I wandered on. Pink lamps made the bacon look appetising and yellow lamps made the butter look rich.

Every now and again I remembered things I needed and wondered how I'd managed to do without. I picked up shoe-laces, writing-paper, ballpens, a wallet – called billfold – the right size for dollars, a motoring magazine, a face-cloth, a shoeshine-outfit and a suede-brush. I also took a carton of corn-fritters because the picture on the box suggested that they were better than potato-chips and because I hadn't tasted corn-fritters before.

About an hour later, the oranges still having eluded me, I found a machine which was swallowing whole oranges, directing the juice into sterilized bottles, fitting the bottles with sterilized caps and disgorging the end-product into a refrigerator. A couple of pints completed my shopping.

Several kindly customers directed me to a cash-up counter, where I emptied my pockets on a conveyor belt. The cashier didn't seem to like my method of carrying goods; she asked rather pointedly whether I was sure I hadn't forgotten anything and advised me to use a trolley next time – like everybody else. By the time I had paid, my purchases had wandered down the conveyor belt and finished up in an enormous brown paper-bag.

I picked it up with a sense of relief. Behind me spread those endless aisles of alien packages, in front of me the plate-glass doors stood open to an ordinary, non-aircon-ditioned, non-neonlighted, sunny day. But as I made for the nearest exit I was horrified to see two lines of shoppers' trolleys converge on me from outside the supermarket. On they came, untouched by human hand, implacably rolling towards my body and my clumsy parcel. *Had* I forgotten to pay for something still in my pocket? Was this retribution? Silently the trolleys slid nearer; there was no doubt they were making for me.

'Hi, Mister!' A boy in monogrammed overalls had come up behind me. 'Do me a favour, will ya? Get off my mag-netic platform ... Gee! Don't you know a simple magnetic strip system when you see one?'

From outside the supermarket it did look simple. The

customers, taking the shopping to their cars, put the trolleys on special strips which automatically returned them to the market.

Back at the dog-show I found Vera waiting at the far end of the judges' table. She was none too pleased with the orange-juice. Drinking from a bottle was out of the question; and of course I'd forgotten to buy cups. As to the perfume, it was at the bottom of the bag.

'For crying out loud,' Vera hissed at me, 'stop scrabbling in this stupid bag. Get rid of it.'

'I bought you...'

'You might have picked a better time for buying shaving-cream. You missed the award.'

The Duke and Grey Rainbow became the centre of a crowd; people agreed that Grey Rainbow deserved the nomination of top-dog in his class; photographers and fanciers took pictures; a girl with a whippet wanted to know whether the *Wee Souls' Sanctuary* would take her animal for training; an exhibitor who owned a bitch asked whether Grey Rainbow was available for breeding. The Duchess told her daughter she'd known from the beginning that her choice was right. She didn't make it clear whether she meant her choice of husband or dog.

Grey Rainbow put up with the scrum patiently until he saw his friend Plato wag his tail and hindquarters. Though the Duke was aware of being pulled into the *Decent Animals Federation* corner he allowed it to happen; it was not the moment for denying his greyhound.

Plato, with a powerful pull against McCall, managed to start a friendly wrestling-match with Grey Rainbow. The liveliness of his play indicated that the effects of the tranquillizing-drug had worn off; he was able and ready to acknowledge his play-mates.

Ben Dryer's movie-camera was whirring away, and the girl with the whippet said wasn't it wild the way these two dogs were having themselves a ball.

My hand, still searching the supermarket-bag, encountered the perfume. While I fished it out, checking the name on the label, I had the impression that Saint Cheetah had got in between Grey Rainbow and Plato. But when I looked up there was no sign of the monkey. What I did notice was that Plato's pants had disappeared.

Meanwhile a loudspeaker was announcing the next part of the show, the judging of the dressed animals' class. Gay Petrell and Sam Bagshott brought forward the dachshunds and Gay's poodles Pip and Solly. Pip objected to having his ears combed and the dachshunds barked in sympathy.

In the middle of the fracas the loudspeaker invited Plato, number eighty-six, to parade before the judges.

Plato's ears went up. He looked at McCall, and he looked at Vera. Then, with sudden resolution, he leaped forward. While McCall stooped to regain Plato's lead the alsatian broke out of the crowd, nudging Vera away from his masters.

'Number eighty-six!' repeated the loudspeaker, somewhat impatiently.

Vera picked up the lead. She glanced at McCall, lifted high her head and marched up to the judges' table.

'Theft,' spluttered McCall. 'Robbery. The shameless hussy .... stealing the clothes off the animal's back. Aye, and parading our dog as if it were her own.'

'It's *your* fault,' said Sam. '*You* let go the dog.'

'Aye, but she's nae business...'

'Quiet, McCall.' Sam was tugging apart the dachshunds who were now snarling at one another. 'I'm not having you goof the whole show.'

'Pardon me,' said Ben Dryer, 'isn't this the clothed animals' class?'

'It is,' Sam told him.

'Then why isn't that alsatian wearing pants?'

'Number eighty-seven,' called the loudspeaker.

Gay stepped forward, with Pip prancing beside her. While Vera, wordlessly, handed over Plato's lead to Sam Bagshot, the judges called Gay up to their table. There was a hush in which Gay and one of the judges became clearly audible.

'... necessary to see him with his pants off,' the judge was saying.

'It's against the rules of our society,' objected Gay.

'Ma'am, it's against *our* rules to pass a dog without being sure that both his testicles are in his scrotum.'

'But the veterinarian examined . . .'

'I don't understand, ma'am. The alsatian we've just seen didn't wear pants. Does your society have one rule for big dogs and another for little dogs?'

'Well, Plato wasn't supposed to be shown without clothes.'

Sam could no longer contain his anxiety. He went to the judges' table and joined in the argument. The judges decided that the D.A.F. dogs would be disqualified unless they could be seen without pants. Sam pointed out that 'clothed animals' class' meant D.A.F. dogs being shown in pants. Then Gay, to the whirring of movie and television cameras, asked whether the judges would allow the D.A.F. dogs to be debagged behind their table and dressed up again for public view. The judges, some amused others exasperated, agreed.

Apart from Gay's Pip and Solly, the dachshunds and Plato, only three other dressed dogs were shown. Each entry after Gay's was discreetly debagged behind the 'counter' and reclothed before being paraded. This new procedure caused a good deal of laughter among the spectators. Only Sam, Gay and McCall managed to look on pokerfaced and unamused.

They looked no happier when the winner of the clothed animals' class was announced. Not surprisingly the award went to the best D.A.F. dog – Plato.

From our corner I could see McCall in acrimonious argument with Sam Bagshot. Then Sam, with apparent reluctance, walked to the judges' table. Almost at once there was an announcement that an objection had been raised.

'What are they doing?' asked Vera. 'They *can't* be asking for a decision against their own dog.'

'They don't want Plato to win,' said Rand. 'He was shown without pants, remember?'

'I don't get it.'

'It's against D.A.F. principles to display animals naked. If they accept Plato's award they're breaking their most important rule.'

'They're nuts.'

'Sure they are.'

Rand was right. It was announced that Plato's award had been withdrawn on owner's demand. Now there was no winner of this class. The D.A.F. contingent gathered its dogs and made for the exit immediately behind us.

McCall stopped in front of Vera. 'That was your doing, woman. Ye'll have a letter from our attorneys.'

'You'll get one from ours if I hear Plato cry at night. There's a society that protects ill-treated animals and . . .'

'Pardon me.' Ben Dryer, movie-camera raised, nudged his way between us. 'I guess you have a real issue here. How about following the proper democratic procedure? If there's an issue I . . .'

'I get it,' said Rand. '*Commies* make threats. In a democracy you discredit your opponent by any means at your disposal.'

'Correct.' Ben took Vera's arm. 'So we talk.'

'The way I see it,' said Ben Dryer, 'such a programme wouldn't do any harm, and it might do a lot of good.'

'To whom?' McCall, oblivious of the comfortable office Ben had secured us, sat on the edge of the chair. 'What good's a public blether to *us*?'

'*Blether?*' inquired Ben.

'Talk.' McCall made it obvious that he didn't think much of a man who didn't know a simple Scots word like blether.

'In the television programme I have in mind the *Decent Animals Federation* as well as the *Wee Souls' Sanctuary* could freely discuss their various training-methods and points of view.'

Sam Bagshot shook his head. 'We have discussed them with . . . our neighbours; to no avail.'

'Aye, they still make Plato disobedient. They still take the clothes off our animals given half a chance. And as to yon young person . . .'

Vera, sweetly, informed McCall of her Christian name.

'Of course,' said Sam Bagshot, 'I have every confidence that a television programme would increase our membership. Deep down people are decent, they're against nakedness.'

'That's true,' McCall agreed. 'But I dinna trust yon people. Mr Dryer says the programme would be unscripted; you canna vouch for what *they'll* be saying.'

'Nothing that's untrue,' Ben assured him. 'I'm sure neither Miss Miller-Hundling nor Mr Morton and Mr Hegel would take advantage of your Federation in a civilized public discussion. Besides you'll have a good, neutral chairman.'

'You?' asked Rand.

'Why, sure; if you wish I'm certain it can be arranged.'

'You remember what *he* said?' asked McCall, jutting out his chin in Rand's direction. 'He admitted he'd try to discredit us.'

'He can't.' There was something rather engaging about Sam Bagshot's faith in his *Decent Animals Federation*.

'They've heard Plato make a rumpus at night.'

'All dogs have a restless night at times, I guess.'

'Well,' McCall at last allowed himself to occupy the whole of his chair. 'Ye can go ahead, Mr Bagshot, but ye've been warned.'

'Miss Miller-Hundling?' asked Ben.

'If my parents aren't opposed ... I guess they won't be ... we'll take part. Okay Rand? Michael?'

'I can't see myself on television,' said Rand. 'I wouldn't kinda ... come over well, would I?'

'Are you going to chicken out?'

'Why no ... no Vera.'

'When would you put us on?' I asked Ben.

'It won't be before next week.'

'I should be returning to England.'

'Gee, you can't,' said Vera. 'Maybe Ben's right ... maybe we'll come to an agreement with the D.A.F. on the programme.' Apparently she hadn't given up the idea of acquiring Plato. 'You want to finish your assignment here, don't you?'

'It *is* finished.'

'Not while there's trouble with McCall and police coming ...'

'I'll thank ye to refer to me as Mr McCall.'

'All right,' I agreed. Perhaps that fierce compatriot of

mine *was* my business.

'There should be three of *us*,' suggested Sam Bagshot. 'Could we have Gay ... Mrs Petrell? She's one of our most loyal supporters.'

'Sure,' said Ben. 'Let's get right down to details.'

CHAPTER TWELVE

'You have di-alled the wrong code. Please replace your receiver and commence from the beginning.' The recorded voice stopped and there was a double click that sounded as if a hostile super-gadget had fastened a padlock over the steel-lips of the girl-automat. What happened if one did *not* replace the receiver? I wanted to know.

The girl-automat's voice came back. 'The telephone company appreciates your co-operation. You have di-alled the wrong code. Please replace...'

There was something about the voice that challenged one to hear its complete performance. After three minutes the automat politely explained that my failure to replace the receiver was causing inconvenience to other subscribers. After six minutes it rebuked me for my asocial behaviour and gave a list of fines for which I'd become liable if I persisted unless, of course, my non-co-operation was due to my sickness or death.

I admitted to myself that I'd been playing with the girl-automat because I was not looking forward to a talk with my girl Julia. Of course I had to put through a transatlantic call, an ordinary letter wasn't going to satisfy Julia at this stage. She had expected me to spend a week in New York. Instead I had already spent two months in the States.

I pulled an armchair to the open french windows of my room and settled down for a long vigil at the telephone. But my second attempt at reaching Julia was disconcertingly successful. Her voice was as loud and clear as if she'd been speaking from Santa Monica.

'Michael, darling! Where are you?'

'Well ... still in California.'

'I see ... You're on your way home?'

'Well, not quite, darling.'

Julia's second 'I see' sounded unfriendly. 'I had a letter from Claire ... Tiger's Claire.'

'Yes? Tiger's play hasn't had much of a run on Broadway. Rather a shame because...'

'Michael!' Julia cut in. 'You forgot to tell me that the Duchess has a family.'

'A couple of youngsters ... Actually I only met one.' I hoped Claire hadn't provided a detailed description of Vera.

'Is *she* in California too?' inquired Julia.

'On and off.'

'More on, I suppose.'

There was a silence. I told Julia not to be silly. 'Look, I'll be home in ten days. We can get married within the month, can't we?'

'Your ... *scientific* papers may not be finished by then.'

'They *are* finished.' I explained why the Alanspring family wished me to stay for the television programme. 'You see, Rand's in practice here. He wouldn't be able to talk as frankly as a vet from another country. I mean, *I* have nothing to lose.'

'Except me.'

'Julia, be reasonable, dear. I think I should see this thing through, no matter how much I miss you.'

'Do you really miss me?'

'Of course, you dope.'

'I know what I'll do!' It sounded ominous. Whenever Julia talked with that positive brightness she was about to commit us to a positive folly.

'Yes?'

'Don't sound so worried, Michael. I'm coming over ... we'll get married and spend our honeymoon in California ... and maybe New Orleans, the Rockies, New York...'

'Julia, you don't realize the distances involved. This isn't just a country; it's pretty well a continent. California is as far from New York as...'

'I know. I'll fly, of course.'

'You'd arrive here on the day I'd be leaving for home.'

'But Michael, you don't *have* to leave ... not if I'm coming to you.'

'Julia, it won't work.' I tried to make it sound firm. 'I've been away two months. We can't expect my uncle to go on doing the work of the practice single-handed.'

'Leave him to me ... I'll send you a wire from New York. See you soon, darling.'

'Julia! Julia!' It was no use. My fiancée had hung up on me.

There was a knock on my door and Vera came in, looking anything but a 'youngster'. 'We're going down to the beach. Coming, Michael?'

'Don't think so. I want to finish my notes on the racoons.'

'You can do that at night.' She perched on the arm of my chair, and kissed me.

'Go and play with Rand.'

'Feeling kinda grounded?'

'No, I just want to work.'

'Rand wants me to marry him.'

'I know. I hope you will.'

'Why?'

'He's just what you need.'

'I guess I don't know *what* I need.'

'Go and find out then.'

'Okay ... so I'm not wanted.' She looked so sad that I found it hard not to contradict her. Fortunately the telephone rang. Masters, at the switchboard, told me Mrs Petrell had been trying to contact me all morning.

'Clifford's playing golf,' Gay explained, self-consciously. With only two out of her eight poodles present the little hotel-apartment appeared bleak compared to her New York home. Gay's unhappy eyes, the mournful music coming over the loudspeaker, the drawn blinds gave the place an aura of disaster.

'Why aren't you on the beach?' I asked.

'I guess one *should* be ... on a holiday,' she said listlessly. 'Oh, Michael! I'm licked.'

'What's happened.'

Instead of answering me she started fussing with an ice-bucket and glasses. She poured us some canned fruitjuice, adding cherries which had been deprived of their stones and stems and fitted with emerald-coloured plastic stems. 'Is this drink okay?'

'Fine.'

'Look.' She pulled open the drawer of an imitation English sofa-table. It was full of dog-clothes, small pants and skirts, sun-bonnets and bows. 'I finished this only yesterday,' she said, holding up a lace-edged skirt. 'I made it myself.' Suddenly she banged the drawer shut. 'Michael, tell me honestly ... is there something wrong ... about dressing up poodles, and about giving them nice clothes?'

'In what sense?'

'Well ... something wrong with me.'

'Gay, I'm a veterinarian, not a doctor.'

'I'm not asking you ... well, not really ... professionally. Just as a friend, and because you're English, like Clifford.'

'What does Clifford think?'

'Please tell me what *you* think. I've got to know.'

'I suppose it *is* a bit childish to dress up your dogs.'

'But *other* people do it.'

'That doesn't make it adult.'

Gay nodded. 'Thanks, Michael. You see ... my first marriage didn't work out. I want this one to last. I got kinda scared.'

'What's worrying you?'

'This morning Clifford said he wished the publicity would stop ... the kind I've been getting. When we got married all the papers quoted me saying I won't visit England while the United Kingdom has those terrible quarantine laws. Well, I just meant I don't want to leave my dogs behind. Then the next thing was Solly's wedding-party and those people taking their clothes off ... *Now* there's the television show. Clifford doesn't want me to take part. He was real nice about it, but he made me feel it was kinda important to him and me that I should give up the *Decent Animals Federation.*'

'You don't *have* to be in on the television programme, Gay.'

'Sam Bagshot would be upset ... on account of the numbers.'

'Well, if it's a question of the *teams* being equal one of *us* can drop out. I'm sure no one will object.'

'I guess you're right. But that's not all. I just know Clifford would like me to take our dogs away from the

D.A.F. and board them with the Duchess while we're abroad.'

'You mean Clifford's altogether against putting animals in clothes?'

'Yes. We had trouble with Solly and Rose after their wedding. Solly just wouldn't go *near* Rose until Clifford made me take their clothes off. I had to let them run around naked for days before they were all right ... I guess it *isn't* the same as it is with people; some animals get kinda miserable if you dress them up.'

'Plato's miserable in pants. Gay, animals are *not* meant to be dressed. Their *fur* serves the purpose of clothes.'

'You think D.A.F. is nuts?'

'Don't you?'

'I don't know any more. When Clifford said *Decent Animals Federation* was like something Tennessee Williams might have dreamed up it made me feel real sick ... I never thought of it that Clifford can look at us ... I mean at Americans ... from the outside. Because he speaks English I didn't think of him as a foreigner. Michael ... I need to know how we appear to foreigners.' Gay's thin, attractive face lifted. She looked at me with the clear perceptive eyes of a child. 'How do *you* feel about us?'

I said, 'That's an impossible question.'

'All right. What do you feel most when you think of us?'

'Pity.'

'You mean you feel *sorry* for us?'

'Not quite. Compassion might be more accurate.' I suddenly realized that I'd told Gay the truth before I myself had consciously formulated it. 'Please don't misunderstand me. There's nothing arrogant or superior about a person who feels compassion for someone ... It simply means that one is touched.'

'What have you in mind? Things like the *Decent Animals Federation*?'

'There are others too, such as the *Sisters of the Tibetan Truth*.'

'Clifford once said to me that organizations like that are symptomatic ... Symptomatic of what?'

'Of a dreadful puritanism ... of personal uncertainties ...

of bewilderment with things unknown such as the world at large...'

'We're the most advanced country in the world,' said Gay.

'Yes, that's *why* it shocks foreigners to find so many terribly human people behind your automats, and computers and space-rockets. *That's* what makes one feel compassion here more than anywhere else.'

'Not dislike?'

'Heaven forbid!'

Gay smiled. 'Do you think we're less adequate as human beings than – say – your people?'

'I don't know.'

'Clifford says the difference between an Englishman and an American is that the Englishman believes he is his brother's keeper; the American is quite sure he *isn't*. If that's true it means we're still irresponsible ... Maybe that's why we need so many taboos and charters ... and societies.'

'Like the *Decent Animals Federation*?'

'Like the D.A.F.; yes. Michael, will you fix me kennels at the Alansprings'?'

'Sure that's what you want?'

'Yes.'

'And the television programme?'

'I'll chicken out of it, somehow.'

Masters met me with the news that a bulldog, accepted the week before, had arrived. The Duke had assigned him the Norman tower folly; Masters felt the dog was still somewhat uncertain whether that splendid structure was a kennel or not.

By the time I visited Ginger, the bulldog had made up his mind what to do with the Norman tower – it obviously was a place meant to be guarded. Ginger received me with a tentative growl modified by tail-wagging. I thought this diplomat of a dog was a little large for the *Wee Souls' Sanctuary* – he was rather a hefty soul.

While I was giving him a routine examination Ginger raised his head and looked towards the top of the hill. In the quiet of the afternoon I too could hear the commotion of snapping branches. It sounded as if a biggish animal was trying to break into the grounds.

Ginger followed me along the fences until we reached the dense hedge of flowering bougainvillaea at the crest. At this spot neither McCall nor ourselves had been able to fix a barrier; the hedge was all of eight feet deep, growing partly on our side partly on D.A.F. land. It should have been a more formidable obstacle to intruders than any man-made fence.

Apparently it wasn't. I saw Grey Rainbow snake his way into the thick of the bougainvillaea, and back out again. While I watched, the greyhound repeated his performance several times. Suddenly I saw Plato's head. The alsatian, led by Grey Rainbow, was burrowing out of the D.A.F. grounds into ours. His big shoulders were pressing back large branches, his powerful front-paws trampling down the undergrowth. Grey Rainbow, thin enough to slip through with ease, kept going back and forth, exploring the thicket, encouraging his playmate.

'He's gonna make it,' said a voice behind me. The boy, who looked like a younger, tougher version of Vera, didn't take his eyes off the dogs. 'I'm Vernon ... Guess you're the English veterinarian. My sister wrote me about you ... You're smart; you don't dig Vera, do you?'

'That's a bit unkind, isn't it?'

'Oh, Vera's great. But I wouldn't dig a dame with all *her* inhibitions ... Gee! He's through!'

Plato, creamy fur somewhat dishevelled, bounded up to me. Suddenly he saw Ginger, standing still and square. Plato, with Grey Rainbow at his side, walked up to the bull-dog step by step. He growled. He gave a deep bark. Ginger didn't budge. He let Plato sniff at him, turned with slow dignity and wandered off in the direction of his Norman tower. Plato went running after him, and presently the two of them returned in perfect amity.

'You aren't going to take him back?' asked Vernon. It seemed his family had kept him informed of their troubles with the *Decent Animals Federation*.

'He *shouldn't* be here.'

'Mother's going to buy him.'

'Our neighbours won't sell.'

'*She'll* get him ... see the ocean?' It was one of the few days when the sea was not obscured by the Los Angeles mists. 'Know something? The first European who recognized the Pacific, as distinct from the Atlantic, was the Spanish explorer Vasco Nunez de Balboa. He discovered its eastern shore from a peak in Panama ... in fifteen-hundred and thirteen ... Where's Vera?'

'Gone swimming.'

'I won't bother. Gotta go back to college at six. Do you play badminton? ... Let's have a game.'

We walked down to the court, the three dogs still with us. Partly to remove Plato from the most visible spot on the estate, partly to find out whether he remembered his training, I whistled the *Stars and Stripes*. Plato vanished instantly.

Vernon played a tough game of badminton. He won the first set, lost the second and wore me out in the third. After that I stopped trying. Vernon was the sort of boy to whom winning mattered.

Between games he kept imparting weird snippets of information. 'Know something? It was Archimedes who discovered displacement ... that's the volume of water displacement when an object floats in it. Archimedes found out about it while he was in his bath. In two hundred and fifty B.C.'

As he walked back to the house Vernon spotted a biggish ship. 'It's a liner,' he said, shielding his eyes. 'Gross tonnage around twenty-nine thousand, I guess. Know something? A passenger sitting inside gives off enough heat to bring twenty-four ounces of water to the boil inside an hour ... or sixty-four ounces if he's moving around fast ... You know how much air circulates through a ship this size in an hour?'

'No.'

'Six-hundred and eighty tons. And the machinery they use to cool the air extracts enough heat to melt thirteen-hundred and fifty tons of ice per day.'

'Where do you find out all these things? At school?'

'No. I kinda like knowing about ships and oceans ... But maybe you're more interested in air. Know something? The atmosphere presses down on the surface of the earth with a weight of about fifteen pounds per square inch ... that's about eighteen tons on someone your size.'

'Vernon!' The Duchess, sitting on the terrace outside the lounge, had heard her son's latest piece of information. 'Vernon, honey, isn't it time you went back to college? Has he exhausted you, Michael? ... When *he's* around my staff just give notice. The cooks I lost because Vernon...'

'Mother,' Vernon pointed to Plato who had made himself comfortable in the shade under the Duchess's chair. 'What are you doing about *him*?'

'He shouldn't be here.' The Duchess dangled her hand and caressed Plato's ears.

'You're just negative, mom. Double your offer for him.'

'Vernon, it's not a question of money. Mr Bagshot has principles.'

'Immature guy.' Vernon looked disgusted. 'Better find somebody who's got principles too, and get him together with Bagshot.'

'Honey, what do you *think* we're doing. *Michael* is here, after all.' Plato suddenly gave a yelp of pain. 'Why ... is there something the matter with his ear?'

There was. At the back of it, close to the head, there was a deep gash. The Duchess had inadvertently pulled off the scab. I thought it necessary to put in a stitch.

Vernon was dissuaded from helping me. He reluctantly climbed into his little MG and took himself off back to college.

Abdul assisted with the operation. Not that it was necessary. Plato was quiet and well behaved when I dealt with his injury. He must have hurt himself during his scramble through the bougainvillaea wilderness.

I might have returned the alsatian to his owners, but when Vera got back from the beach she swung opinion in favour of Plato. The dog had put up with enough that day. Didn't he look comfortable? Wouldn't it be awful to hear him cry through the night? 'Consequences?' she said. 'Never mind about consequences. As Vernon always says, "to hell with poverty! put another pea in the soup!"'

I thought we were putting a perilous number of peas in this particular soup.

Sam Bagshot and McCall were becoming more patient, probably because they were chary of upsetting a television programme from which they promised themselves a big increase of membership. Plato had been with us three days before the *Decent Animals Federation* took action.

The emissaries, Attorney Blick and a police-officer who had visited us before, arrived while we were having tea on the terrace. Blick scanned the garden, looked relieved on not seeing Plato around and began to tell us how distressed Mr Bagshot was to have lost his dog again. Were we certain we hadn't seen the alsatian?

'We have so many dogs here,' said the Duchess, with superb vagueness.

The policeman asked permission to look over the grounds.

'Jeremiah will show you round,' said Vera. Jeremiah could be heard swinging *Oh Lord our help in ages past* behind a nearby rose bed. Vera went to fetch him. 'Jeremiah, have you seen the alsatian?' she asked the gardener.

'No, ma'am.'

'Will you go look for him with the police-officer?'

'Yes, ma'am, but . . .'

'Thanks.' Vera knew that Plato would keep out of Jeremiah's way. The gardener had once inadvertently doused him with his hose; besides Plato seemed to dislike his rendering of hymns – or rather, of the only hymn Jeremiah bothered to sing.

Mr Blick accepted a cup of lemon-tea. 'My client's real upset. The lady who was to take part in the television discussion has let him down . . . Well, she gave health-reasons. But the result's the same; a . . . er . . . disbalance in the programme, unless *you* can see your way to a slight change of plans. Mrs Petrell suggested we should talk to you.'

'What do you have in mind?' asked the Duchess.

'If your side didn't have a lady-speaker either . . .'

'Just four speakers.' Vera sounded surprisingly mild. 'I guess I'd agree to drop out if *Mr Bagshot* is reasonable.'

'Quite right,' agreed the Duke. 'Can't have dealings with a fellow who keeps sending policemen to one's place.'

'My client won't trouble you again,' promised Mr Blick. 'Not before the television show. Naturally he can't allow that dog to go ... all over the place indefinitely without taking ... some action.'

'Tell your client,' said Vera, 'we still want to buy Plato ... if he can find the dog.'

'I'm sure my client wouldn't contemplate selling Plato ... certainly not *before* the show.'

The polite blackmailing continued until Jeremiah and the police-officer returned. The alsatian *had* kept out of sight.

'We'll *get* Plato,' said Vera, watching the visitors drive away.

'Wouldn't be too sure,' the Duke warned her. 'That fellow Bagshot's a fanatic. Can't trust the type.'

'If we handle it right he'll *have* to let go Plato. I've got an idea.' Vera opened her handbag. 'Look, here's an advertisement of the television programme. I cut it out of Jackie's film-magazine ... Gee!' she pulled out an envelope. 'Michael, I'm sorry. I forgot to give it to you.'

A cable. 'When did it arrive?'

'In the morning.'

It was from Julia. She'd landed in New York.

CHAPTER THIRTEEN

Julia in America. It made me feel that Vernon's information had been pretty accurate – the atmosphere *was*
pressing down on me with a weight of eighteen tons. I'd
have looked forward to Julia's arrival if her reaction to Vera
had not been so predictable. Julia would take one look and
decide that Vera had been the reason for my prolonged stay
in America.

She'd be wrong, of course. I had stayed because I had
become interested in a country which seemed to me stranger, more outlandish than the remotest parts of Europe.
What had seduced me was not young Vera but the perpetual surprise of meeting people who spoke the same
language as I without having anything in common with
other English-speaking people I'd known. In France, Italy
or Spain I'd been a visitor who didn't know much of the
local languages, but I had *not* felt an alien.

In America I did feel an alien. It was a new sensation,
puzzling, disturbing yet always intriguing. But how was I to
convince Julia? – Julia who immediately felt sceptical whenever I gave an indication of being interested in anything
other than football, animals and women.

I realized that Vera, treating me with her normal, casual
familiarity, would inevitably create the wrong impression.
Julia would sense at once that I had not talked of her as
much as a devoted fiancé should. I *was* devoted to Julia. I
wanted to marry her. I hadn't forgotten that horrible
winter when Julia, jealous of Claire, had gone to ground;
the very idea of another such separation depressed me. How
was I to prevent it?

I spent the night in silent monologue, composing justifi-
cations and arguments with which to convince Julia of my
innocence. I worried and tossed about, with the mocking-
birds' monotonous call dinning in my ears, listening to the
coyotes whining and the racoons tearing at my screen-

doors. Too weary to get up and pacify them with apples and cookies I let them do their worst. At dawn I went to sleep – or rather into a no-man's-land of surrealist nightmares.

But in the morning I knew what was needed to save my impending marriage. It was Tuesday. Julia's plane was due at the International Airport on Thursday, about the time Rand and I would arrive at the television studios. I had less than two days and two nights in which to make Vera and Rand look and behave like a couple of lovers.

'I don't know why it is, Vera,' said Rand, 'but your ideas are always off-beat. They're kinda unethical.'

'You *would* see it that way.' Vera rolled over in the sand, and gazed at a screwed-up newspaper which was lazily rolling along the beach. 'How do you propose fixing Sam and McCall if you don't know what they're going to say at the show?'

'We'll take a chance.'

'That's just soft ... But I guess you're the wrong guy for finding out what they have in mind. You'd make such a noise you'd get yourself arrested.'

'I say,' Abdul abruptly stopped his contemplation of the ocean. 'If you really want to go ahead with your scouting *I* am the fellow to do it. Queer thing ... I've been away from India for donkey's years but I still move more silently than a European.'

'Why, that's true,' agreed Vera. 'Would you *do* it, Abdul?'

'Well – as Rand points out – it's hardly playing the game. On the other hand Bagshot and McCall are bound to discuss what they're going to say on television ... and it *would* be a pity if we didn't know beforehand. Actually I'm absolutely against spying on people, except when there's a principle involved. In this case there *is*. I'm dead against putting animals in clothes ... my *doctrine* makes that abundantly clear.'

'Then you'll do it?'

'Yes, I really think I should.'

'You'll get in okay,' said Rand, 'but how are you going to *stay* in? Those dachshunds are going to bark.'

'They always bark,' Vera pointed out.

'Not at night.'

Abdul waved an elegant brown hand. 'No need to worry about their dogs. I have a theory about them.'

Rand looked worried. 'Sure, but will that stop them yapping?'

'Well, Harry MacMillan used to say one must have freedom to improvise. If necessary I'll improvise on the basis of my theory.'

'That's settled then,' said Vera. 'But you won't be able to meet Julia at the airport.'

'I don't see why not.' Abdul sounded disappointed. Apparently he looked forward to *anyone* from England.

'Don't you see? They'll probably finalize their talk just before they're off to the studios ... I guess my stepfather had better meet Michael's friend.'

Perhaps I should have corrected 'friend' with 'fiancée', but I didn't. Though Vera had taken the news of Julia's arrival quite well, I couldn't trust her; she had a talent for mischief. Rand was right; when Vera had an 'idea' it was more often than not unethical.

That night I heard someone creep past beneath my balcony. It was hours after we had dispatched Abdul, in black levis and sweater, to the grounds of the *Decent Animals Federation*.

For once I was certain that the prowler was human, not animal. Presently I heard the baritone-bark of Ginger. I got up, put on jeans and shirt and picked up the flashlight I'd kept in my room ever since Plato's nocturnal escape.

The night was black, and – it seemed to me – more imbued with savagery than nights in Europe. In the dark the racoons, charming little clowns at other times, attacked one another over scraps of garbage; sleepy lizards were devoured by boas and rattle-snakes; the coyotes combed the hillside for the lairs of fawns and does; owls hunted bats and the grey foxes went stalking the harmless king-snake. There were dozens of suspicious noises. And if one managed to avoid the predatory animals there were always the poisonous plants which could do as much damage as an animal-bite.

Half-way up the hill I struck the brook which had a reputation for inundating the gardens during wet seasons. Since
I had been staying at *The Cottage* the stony runnel had
been dry; the only evidence that it occasionally carried
water was a patch of mud at the foot of some sycamore
trees. A high branch of one of those trees supported an
enormous, solid curtain of silver-rimmed ivy.

As I stood, listening, the tree groaned like a man – an
uncanny sound. I decided to tell Jeremiah that the branch
was dying off; if it fell, weighted as it was with all that ivy,
it could cause a bad accident.

There was another groan, and presently a curious squelch-
ing noise. It sounded like a large animal's wallowing in the
mud, having a bath. I didn't think a creature that size
would be *stranded*; the mire was hardly deep enough.

I parted the curtain of ivy and shone my light in the
direction of the sounds. The man who had been in the mud
shot upright.

'Who's there?' asked Rand. He sounded uncommonly
aggressive.

'It's me.'

'What are *you* doing out here, Michael?'

'I thought McCall was prowling.'

Rand laughed. 'His mind wouldn't work along Vera's
lines. He's another kinda nut.' He wiped his hands on a
handkerchief, and put on a pair of tennis-shoes. 'I feel great
... Let's have a drink. I've got some bourbon in my room.'

He strode off at a fast pace, recklessly ignoring the pos-
sibilities of treading on a snake or brushing against poison-
oak. And all he was wearing beside his shoes was a pair of
shorts.

When we got to his room, it became apparent that he *had*
been rolling in the mud. He was covered in the stuff. He
poured our drinks and then fetched a towel which he spread
on the carpet.

'I feel great.' He sat down on the towel and crossed his
legs buddha-fashion. 'You should try it some time.'

'What? Wallowing in the mud?'

'Sure. That's what we need ... all of us. We need to get

filthy dirty without giving a damn. Get rid of that stupid puritanism. Get rid of our inhibitions. Get the feel of good decent earth on us.'

'Is that an Abdul-doctrine?'

'Abdul hasn't begun to understand our special problem here. The guy who worked it out is Dr Korenski ... an alienist.'

'You consulted him?'

Rand didn't answer that. 'The trouble goes right back to one's childhood ... growing up in *nice* neighbourhoods, mothers who always do things right, parents who see you do everything exactly like everyone else in the neighbourhood. If you fall in the dirt ... why, you take a shower and put on clean clothes before you let anyone see you; and if you want sex you make sure *no one* sees you.'

'That doesn't sound all that abnormal to me.'

'It is ... if you're brought up to believe that cleanliness equals holiness, and sex equals dirt and therefore sin.'

'So the mud's been a ... liberating experience?'

'Sure. You get into it and you find out it's great ... nothing wrong with it ... nothing at all.'

I had a vision of Rand wrecking my future as well as his own. 'Look here, if I were you I wouldn't say these things to Vera. Don't think she'd see it Dr Korenski's way. Mud may be pleasant and ... liberating, but making love is pleasant and liberating in quite another fashion. Vera wouldn't like it if you put on a par your mud-baths and making love to her ... And *don't* call it having sex.'

'So she's discussed it with you?' Something of Rand's usual moroseness had got into his eyes.

'I wouldn't call it a discussion. She just told me that she dislikes that particular phrase.'

'Thanks, Michael.' Rand looked happier. 'I'm sure glad you told me ... Vera's not like other girls. She's smart.'

'Very attractive too. Ben Dryer thinks she's a honey.'

'The television producer?'

'Of course. He's phoned her every day since we met.'

'She didn't tell me.'

'Why should she?' I got up. It seemed a good moment to leave Rand to further psychological reflections.

*

I did not hear Rand go out on the following night. But around one in the morning Abdul wakened me by switching on the lights.

'I say, what's going on?' He sat down on my bed, and lit a cigarette. 'What does Rand think he's doing?'

'Why?'

'It's rather weird. I saw him walk in from the garden covered in mud. He was practically naked.'

'No trousers?'

'Just a towel ... Not even shoes. Bit dangerous that. What's it in aid of?'

'It's all right. He has a theory.'

'Oh, I see.' Abdul was satisfied with my explanation. 'I suppose it's all right? ... I watched him.'

'What happened.'

'He washed and changed.'

'That's reasonable enough.'

'Then he went into Vera's room.'

'And was thrown out?'

'Well, no ... at least, not while I kept an eye on her door.'

'How long was that?'

'About half an hour, I suppose. I say, I wish you wouldn't mention this to anyone.'

'Of course I won't.'

'You see my point, don't you Michael? I mean, it's not on ... watching people, is it. I wouldn't have ... only Rand looked rather peculiar in that dirty towel. I thought he might be ill.'

'I'm sure he isn't ... You're back early, aren't you?'

'Well, there was no point in hanging around. McCall and Bagshot had a sort of dress-rehearsal. I have a pretty good idea how they're going to play it on television.'

CHAPTER FOURTEEN

The day of the show. I could concentrate on nothing but Julia's imminent arrival; Rand appeared to be day-dreaming of Vera; Vera anticipated the television programme by reiterating Ben Dryer's possible questions and everyone's likely answers. And Abdul kept saying he couldn't understand why he'd given so much of his time to the *Wee Souls' Sanctuary*; it wasn't as if its inception had entailed much work. As soon as I was gone he'd rough out a new doctrine; he'd have to get down to it or California would get *him* down.

The Duke told the Duchess anecdotes of Julia. Capital girl Julia ... former Indian Army officer's daughter ... brought up with snakes ... frightfully good with cobras ... used to do a snake-dance in Soho ... helped old Michael catch a horse-doper once.

'That was at Kempton Park,' elaborated the Duke.

The Duchess fed Plato a lump of sugar from the tea-table. 'Abdul says McCall's been talking of sending him to New York.'

'Who?'

'Plato.'

'Shady character, that Sidney ... sort of fellow who *would* interfere with horses.'

'I just know New York would kill him.'

'Cunning too. Wouldn't give the dope to the horses himself.'

'Willard, if *they* try to take him to New York we must call the anti-cruelty society.'

'Know what he did? Gave the stuff to the owner ... nice old thing who thought she was giving her horses sugar.'

'But I guess the television programme will make them think. They'll be *news*. Maybe they won't dare provoke publicity over Plato.'

'Publicity, I'm in favour of it. Only thing to do ... expose fellows who dope animals.'

'Why, Willard! You don't think they've been giving him tranquillizers again, do you?'

'Who?'

'Plato.'

'Oh ... er ... I've been talking about Julia; you know, Michael's girl. Time to go to the airport, I suppose. Must put on a tie.'

'Hurry, Rand!' shouted Vera, slamming the door of his car. 'We'll be late.'

'Plenty of time,' I tried to reassure her.

'Abdul,' Vera grabbed hold of Saint Cheetah, 'you're *not* taking this monkey?'

'She could stay in the car.'

'No.'

'She'll make a nuisance of herself if I leave her behind.'

'Jackie will look after her.'

'Saint Cheetah's scared of Jackie's fingernails.'

'It'll be good for her ... the monkey, I mean. She *needs* training.'

'That's interesting, Vera. You do actually believe in using fear as a method of enforcing discipline. I've been considering this question in the context of my new doctrine. Burke classifies fear as one of the passions ... "No passion so effectually robs the mind of all its powers of acting and reasoning as fear" ... Assuming you pose this theory...'

'Rand!' Vera was almost in tears.

He came sprinting out of the house. 'Okay honey, okay.'

'Have you got enough gasoline?'

'Sure.'

'Got the notes I gave you?'

Both Rand and I palpated our pockets.

'No,' said Rand. 'But we aren't going to use notes.'

'Gee!' Vera sighed. '*Tak*e them. You might want to read them through before the show.'

'Okay.'

Rand was about to leave the car, but Vera caught him by the tail of his coat. 'Not *you*. Michael, you'd better find them ... please.'

When I got back Vera was still quizzing Rand; had he remembered to check the oil? Did we have water in the radiator? Had Saint Cheetah mussed her dress?

'You look great, honey.'

'Better avoid Sunset Boulevard,' said Vera.

'But that's the fastest way.'

'Not now. You'll run into traffic leaving the beach.'

'You wanna drive?' Rand sounded aggressive.

Oddly enough Vera subsided. But it wasn't the kind of giving-way that happens between lovers. Too petulant. Whatever had happened between these two the night before had not improved Vera's manner towards Rand. I had failed, Julia would walk in on us and my position would look to her thoroughly equivocal.

Our nose-to-tail crawl to the television-studios made me feel trapped, depressed, almost as morose as a Californian or a Russian. Had anyone told me a story of someone drowning in the Volga I too would have laughed myself to death.

At the studios a secretary, with fingernails almost as long as Jackie's, led us to the make-up rooms. The thought that the secretary had probably bought Jackie's nails cheered me up.

Ben Dryer came striding in, bending over my grease-paint covered face. 'I've put Sam Bagshot and McCall next door. Can't have you get together before the show ... What I want is a real hard argument ... just the way you feel deep down.'

The quiet of the studio, the cameras being handled by casual, gum-chewing technicians soon made me forget that a few million people would see it if I scratched my nose or McCall jerked his bagpipe-arm. There was a workaday atmosphere not so different from the dissecting-room of the Veterinary College.

'... so that two distinctly different methods of animal-training have arrived in California,' Ben Dryer was saying. 'The methods of Mr Morton and Mr Hegel could be described as the British system ... it's based on the doctrine of Abdul Karim Kochbar ... Mr Hegel, er ... Rand, what would you say is the basis of your method?'

'Well, the best way of making an animal behave as *you* want is to hold out promises.'

'Mr Morton ... Michael, doesn't that amount to a system of bribery?'

'It's common sense,' I said. 'If an animal isn't rewarded for good behaviour it'll understand even less than humans why it should do as it's told.'

'What do you do in cases of bad behaviour.'

'Find out, whenever possible, the reason for it,' said Rand. 'That means we rarely have to punish an animal.'

'But you don't exclude punishment.'

'Certainly not. Young animals especially have to be handled with firmness.'

'Reactionary,' muttered McCall.

'Sam Bagshot,' Ben pointedly ignored the kennel-manager, 'Sam, would you tell us in what way your system varies from the Abdul doctrine?'

'Above all,' said Sam, 'we don't hold out any promises. Our relationship with animals is based on mutual respect and – above all – decency.'

'Would you elaborate that, Sam?'

'Why, sure. My feeling's always been that we don't properly respect animals. If we did we wouldn't let them run around like savages ... naked. It makes the animal feel kinda exposed – which sets up psychological complexes – and it puts dangerous ideas into the heads of little children.'

'Aye.' McCall nodded his head. 'And *adults.*'

'And adults,' agreed Sam. 'What could be more indecent than a couple of dogs mating right in the middle of a respectable park. That's the kind of horror I've seen with my own eyes ... in Central Park, New York. Now, what would be the effect on a child of such a spectacle.'

'It might become a nice natural adult,' said Rand.

Sam chose not to hear. 'The child will grow up obsessed with sex. Nor is the damage confined to kids. Think of the unlucky motorist, driving along safely, suddenly confronted with a naked cow! Immediately his mind gets confused and he's safe no longer. The *Decent Animals Federation* have just institooted a survey to bring out into the open the number of motor-accidents caused by shock on seeing a naked animal.'

'Isn't that a costly project?' asked Ben.

'Our funds have risen to close on two million dollars. I guess that proves how much the problem of indecent animals is in people's minds.'

'I believe you have an active system for dealing with indecency.'

'We certainly have. All members of D.A.F. are pledged to put their animals in clothes ... at least a pair of comfortable shorts.'

'What if a dog wants to use a tree?' asked Rand. 'A tree's a great thing for a dog.'

'Stretch-nylon,' said Sam. 'But, in fact, we don't encourage dogs to use trees ... As the animals get used to a more civilized way of life they'll acquire a better control over ... er ... natural functions.'

'Now, here's a real important question.' Ben glanced towards the door. 'Don't dogs resist being put into pants?'

'Why, they *like* it.'

'How can you tell, Sam?'

'Easy. You show those pants to a dog, and he wags his tail right away.'

'That's a little hard to believe ... I think, Sam, you should demonstrate what you've been telling us.'

'That'll be a real pleasure.' The secretary had appeared at the door with the two D.A.F. dachshunds on a lead.

'As it happens,' Ben smiled into the nearest camera, 'we have a couple of little dogs right here in the studio.'

Rand and I looked at one another. So far Sam's tactics had been what we'd expected. Even Abdul's report of the dachshunds' appearance had been accurate.

San and Ben lifted them on to the table. Both dogs looked docile and somewhat sleepy. It was hard to tell whether they'd been dosed with tranquillizers or not.

'Tate and Lyle,' McCall introduced them. He pulled a pair of stretch-pants from his pocket and showed them to the dogs. Tate immediately began to move his tail from side to side, rather like a clockwork-animal. Lyle hesitated, but eventually did produce a mild tail-wag.

'You see,' said Sam, while McCall got the dogs' hind-quarters into the trews, 'they're real crazy about wearing pants.'

As McCall returned the dogs to the secretary I got a distinctive whiff of stewed meat.

'That was remarkable,' I congratulated Sam. 'Obviously small dogs don't object to being put in pants. But how would a large dog react?'

'Exactly the same.' Sam looked pleased with himself. 'Our experience is that there's no difference ... none at all.'

'I take it your alsatian is keen on wearing pants?'

Sam glanced at me. 'Sure. After an initial training period *all* dogs prefer to be decently dressed.'

'How long, would you say, is this initial training period?'

'Six months.'

'Or longer?'

'No, six months at most.'

'Mr Bagshot,' Rand said, mildly, 'you *have* an alsatian, haven't you.'

McCall drew himself up. 'Aye, and ye've caused...'

'Yes,' said Sam, firmly, 'I have an alsatian.'

'How old is he?' asked Rand.

'We're no here to discuss yon dog,' interjected McCall.

Ben Dryer raised his hand. 'I guess Rand's mentioned the alsatian for a purpose ... We want to hear a little more about the reactions of large dogs, since we haven't got one in the studio. Now, Rand, you asked how old Sam's alsatian is, didn't you?'

'He's three,' said Sam.

'You've trained him in your usual way?'

'Why, yes.'

'He too wears those pants?'

'He does.'

'I'd be real interested to see Mr McCall put pants on so large an animal,' said Rand.

At this point Plato appeared in the door. Vera, as we'd planned, had put him on a long lead so that she herself remained invisible.

'Perhaps,' Rand looked at Ben, 'it would be possible to

fetch the alsatian. I believe he accompanied Sam to the studios.'

'Well ... no. That is ...' Sam's face showed so much embarrassment that I felt sorry for him.

'Yon dog's not here,' said McCall.

'Isn't he?' Rand managed his fake-astonishment very well.

At this point even McCall began to realize that we meant to produce Plato. 'And I'll tell ye why he isn't here,' spluttered McCall. 'Mr Bagshot's sold him.'

'To friends,' said Sam, shakily.

'I see.' I felt I had to put him out of his misery. 'He's gone to his new owners ... no doubt some distance from here.'

'That's right.' Sam was recovering his poise. 'I'm sure sorry we're unable to show you the alsatian. He's a great dog. I sure hated parting with him, but he's gone to a family who have kids ... and Plato's kinda crazy about kids. Our policy's *happy animals*. And there's no doubt in my mind that animals – like people – are happiest when they're decently covered.'

'Thank you, Sam Bagshot,' said Ben. 'Now, we've just a minute left so I'd like to hear a word from our guest from England. Michael, what's been your impression of pets in the States? Are they as well bred?'

'Certainly they are.'

'And animal owners?'

'Even those that have bats in the belfry take good care of their pets.'

It was fortunate that the cameras chose that moment for panning to a girl with a cookie-advertisement.

McCall would have started a brawl if Sam hadn't put himself between us. 'Slander!' he shouted. 'It was downright slander. Ye'll no take a public insult from yon young devil, will ye, Mr Bagshot?'

'There was no insult intended,' Ben tried to pacify him. 'I'd say Michael wished to end up on a conciliatory note.'

'Aye, but the implication was that we're mad.'

'If that's so,' Sam looked rather worried, 'I certainly won't hesitate to sue Mr Morton.'

154

'Now just ye repeat what ye said,' demanded McCall.

'I *heard* it,' said Vera. 'Michaél said, even those people who have vets in the belfry take good care of their pets.'

'He said, *bats*,' insisted McCall.

Ben shook his head. 'No, I'm certain it was *vets*.'

'Rubbish. *Vets* in the belfry doesn't mean anything; bats certainly does.'

'You're wrong, Mr McCall,' said Vera, sweetly. 'I heard the expression "vets in the belfry" quite often when I was in England ... I guess you've lived in the States a long time, so you're out of touch. Vets in the belfry means kinda ... keeping vets in reserve. Like us, when we started the *Wee Souls' Sanctuary*. My mother would never have opened our kennels without veterinarians being right there on the estate. Vets in the belfry means ... well, you keep the veterinarian right close in case one of your animals gets sick. My stepfather's cousin in Scotland keeps Irish setters and ...'

McCall suddenly looked interested. 'The Duke's cousin wouldna be Sir Angus McNabb?'

'Why sure.'

McCall was too shrewd to believe someone such as Vera, but a good look at Sam Bagshot convinced him that he'd better accept the proffered face-savers. 'Then we'll say no more about it,' he grunted.

'Mr Bagshot,' Vera opened her purse. 'I've got the cheque for Plato right here.'

'That was a downright dishonest...' McCall's temper was rising again.

Sam grabbed the cheque. 'Sure, I'll take it ... In my opinion Plato will give you a lot of trouble if...'

'Julia!' She was standing in the doorway, beside the Duke. And her hairdo looked exactly like Vera's. What could have been more unfortunate? As I tried to kiss her she turned, so that my lips barely brushed her cheek. She hadn't taken her eyes off Vera.

'Had a good journey, darling?' I asked.

'Yes, thank you.' It sounded stiff.

'How was New York?'

'New York.'

'Julia . . .'

'Yes, Michael?'

'Oh, honey!' I heard Vera. Somehow she'd arrived in Rand's arms. 'Honey, you were great!'

Julia, rather uncertainly, let me take her hand.

'Gee, the way you said, "Mr Bagshot, you have an alsatian, haven't you?" It sure got me . . . You don't mind, Michael, do you? Rand . . . Well . . . he gave me that psychological feeling. I guess *you* just don't.'

THE ORIGINAL BESTSELLING VET BOOKS

by

Alex Duncan

IT'S A VET'S LIFE
THE VET HAS NINE LIVES
VETS IN THE BELFRY

A true and outrageously funny series concerning the exploits of veterinary surgeon Michael Morton, the animals in his care, and the owners the animals really owned.

'What Richard Gordon has done for doctors, Alex Duncan is doing for vets.' BOOKS AND BOOKMEN

'The author's fast and furious pace never conceals a hard core of veterinary experience.' THE COUNTRYMAN

'See how the Richard Gordon formula works just as successfully with animals.' PHILIP OAKES

'*Vets in the Belfry* is like its predecessors – or even more so – very funny indeed.' CATHOLIC HERALD

'Alex Duncan looks like becoming the Richard Gordon of the animal clinics.' LONDON EVENING NEWS

ALIDA BAXTER

FLAT ON MY BACK
UP TO MY NECK
OUT ON MY EAR

The hilarious saga in which Alida Baxter gets to the root of what living and loving in the '70s is all about – entirely dismembering her husband, sex and marriage . . .

'The funniest books I've read for years.' GOOD HOUSE-KEEPING

'In the long line of a writing tradition that includes Richard (Doctor in the House) Gordon, and James (Let Sleeping Vets Lie) Herriot . . . wholly worthwhile entertainers.' SMITH'S TRADE NEWS

'Ms. Baxter does a most difficult thing very well. She makes her life not only funny but interesting.' DAILY MIRROR

'Her honeymoon, a move to Germany, in-laws, out-laws – Alida treats them all like a slide on a banana skin. The result is just as hilarious.' ANNABEL

'Hilariously funny.' OVER 21

'Happily recommended.' FORUM

'Smiles all the way.' BOOKS AND BOOKMEN

THE MARX BROS. SCRAPBOOK

Groucho Marx and
Richard J. Anobile

'Virtually all the beans are spilled . . . What rich and fascinating material it is.' NEW YORK MAGAZINE

'The best record of the family's life . . . uninhibited not to say earthy when Groucho lets the language rip.' DAILY MIRROR

'A treasure-trove for Marx Brothers fans and for movie-goers generally . . . This is a remarkable book, a funny book, and one to read through again and again.' WHAT'S ON

'The all-time definitive work on the subject. A collector's item . . . A classic.' CHICAGO SUN-TIMES

'No true Marx Brothers buff will be without it.' YORKSHIRE POST

'Compelling gossip.' THE TIMES

'Hugely enjoyable . . . It's especially good to see Groucho at 83 in such candid and caustic form.' OXFORD MAIL

This is the controversial, 'scandalous', beguiling and absolutely authentic memoir of the most famous foursome in movie history, recounted by none other than the master himself. With 300 splendid illustrations and memorabilia to bring you for the first time, *the one, the only, the real Marx Bros.*

75p

STAR BOOKS

are available through all good
booksellers but, where difficulty is encountered,
titles can usually be obtained *by post* from:

Star Book Service,
G.P.O. Box 29,
Douglas,
Isle of Man,
British Isles.

Please send retail price plus 8p per copy.

Customers outside the British Isles should
include 10p post/packing per copy.

Book prices are subject to alteration without notice.